PRAISE FOR CINDY PROCTER-KING

"Cindy Procter-King is a master storyteller. Not only do her characters invite the readers into the drama, the humor is non-stop. Comedy is a hard genre to write but Cindy Procter-King does it easily."

— THE ROAD TO ROMANCE ON HEAD OVER HEELS

"What a set-up for a comedy of errors! Everything that can go wrong in this scenario does go wrong, and the reader is well entertained by the comedic chaos. If you like your romance with humor, you'll love this one."

— FALLEN ANGEL REVIEWS ON HEAD OVER HEELS

"I really enjoyed Borrowing Alex. It was smart and funny without being overdone. The characters do some pretty funny things in the name of love. I am definitely looking forward to reading the next book I find by Cindy Procter-King."

— JOYFULLY REVIEWED ON BORROWING ALEX

"I really like romantic comedy as a genre, but it takes some really good writing to make me laugh. This book made me laugh."

"Cindy Procter-King presents readers with a suspenseful snapshot of a romantic comedy... If you like your suspense stories a little on the gritty side but loaded with humor, this is a must-read."

"Procter-King has written a 'home' for all of us. Destiny Falls is the place that holds your first love, your first triumph; it's where you lost a person you cared about. Jess is a character who women will identify with, having to forget a past that is beyond difficult to do."

GETTING OVER
Brett

ALSO BY CINDY PROCTER-KING

Love in the Pacific Northwest

Sassy Romance

Head Over Heels

Borrowing Alex

Sassy Suspense

Picture Imperfect

Destiny Falls

Contemporary Romance

Where She Belongs

Love and Other Calamities

Short Fiction

Deceiving Derek

Catching Claire

GETTING OVER *Brett*

CINDY PROCTER-KING

Blue Orchard Books

GETTING OVER BRETT

Copyright © 2018 Cindy Procter-King

This is a work of fiction. The characters and events in this book are of the author's imagination and are not to be construed as real. Any resemblance to actual incidents or persons, living or dead, is coincidental and not intended by the author.

Published in Canada by Blue Orchard Books

www.blueorchardbooks.com

ISBN: 978-0-9936794-9-0

Digital: 978-0-9936794-5-2

Editor, Karen Block

Cover Design, The Killion Group

To Allie McBeagle, my office companion and walking buddy of 16 years. RIP, beaglah-girl.

 *ori's To-Do List ~ Sunday*

- *Take down wall paneling*
- *Check on hurt helper guy*
- *If opportunity knocks, slam the door*

HAND ON THE doorknob, Brett Evans stood just inside the closed front door in the partly demolished living room of his childhood friends, Ryan and Tori Jarrett. Sheets of old wall paneling lay stacked against a baseboard. Pink sweatpants hugged Tori's rear as she climbed a stepladder. Music blared from a cell phone docked in a boom box. Tori sang along with gusto, a light brown ponytail poking out the back of her scruffy baseball cap.

Bile churned in Brett's gut. The last time he saw Tori's curvy behind, she was yanking on a pair of silky white panties while he explained why they could never sleep together again. Their conversation hadn't gone too well.

Four years had passed since he'd committed the unthinkable

and taken her virginity the night of her brother's wedding. Tori was his best friend's little sister, twenty-two at the time, and saving herself for the right man.

But Brett hadn't known any of that.

He wouldn't have slept with her had he known.

Had she *told* him.

Releasing a breath, he set his laptop case on the carpet and adjusted the cuffs of his button-down shirt. Whoever said or did what the night Ry got married no longer mattered. He was here now. He'd say hi, and Tori would either greet him with her beautiful smile or bare those perfect white teeth never touched by an orthodontist and bite off his head.

Brett sawed his jaw back and forth. Was he ready for this confrontation so soon after arriving? Sure, he'd expected to run into Tori during the four weeks of his software consulting contract with a Portland manufacturing firm. Maybe two or three days after he had settled in with her folks.

But not yet. And certainly not within the next ten seconds.

Clearing his throat, he stepped closer.

Tori remained focused on her work, singing about mad love and bad blood as she retrieved a nail puller from an insanely sexy tool belt slung low on her hips. With a quick twist of her wrist, she pried the upper portion of paneling off the wall studs. Moments before, when Brett entered the 1930s bungalow, she'd just loosened the panel's other side. Now the painted wood creaked as tiny nails popped free. A couple at the bottom remained pinned.

Tori emitted a satisfied-sounding grunt. After hooking the nail puller onto her tool belt, she tugged with gloved hands until the nails loosened. The panel crashed to the floor.

"Another one bites the dust!" she cheered above the music, pumping a fist in a victory thrust.

Brett swallowed a smile.

The stepladder wobbled. Her left foot slipped. "Yikes!" She

grabbed the top rung. "That's right, moron, kill yourself, why don't you? Leave poor Rex all alone. Real nice."

Rex? Brett's stomach clenched. Had Tori finally found Mr. Right?

"Tori?" he called.

She turned and screamed.

ॐ

Tori Jarrett gripped her father's old stepladder, heart racing like a herd of stampeding elephants. What the hell was Brett Evans doing in her living room?

"Seriously, Evans! Don't you knock?" she yelled above the country-rap remix filling her comfy house. "You almost scared me to death."

Curse her rotten luck! In her ancient sneakers, sweats, and a grimy white T-shirt, she must look like she'd crawled out of a trashcan. Not the effect she'd wanted to project if she'd ever possessed the bad karma to see Brett Evans again.

She'd wanted to look incredibly desirable and sexy and basically so un-Tori-like that he would regret with every fiber of his being having river-danced all over her heart before disappearing to California four years ago.

But, as usual, Brett had surprised her.

His hands shot up. "Sorry." With his neatly trimmed blond hair and killer blue eyes, he was still so handsome it annoyed her. "Is your mom around?" he shouted.

"Look, Brett, it doesn't matter." Tori hopped off the ladder and shed her leather work gloves, tossing them to the carpet. Her *Keep Portland Weird* hat would stay on. Call it bad timing, accursed coincidence, or an ironic fluke of fate, but she hadn't washed her hair this morning. The stifling end-of-May heat wave becoming more common in her beloved and usually drizzly Pacific Northwest had plastered several strands to her skull.

"Can I turn this down?" Brett's trousers creased in interesting places as he moved to the music player inches away.

A whiff of sandalwood drifted to Tori's nostrils. *Yi-yi*, the man smelled delicious. Turning thirty hadn't diminished his charisma one iota. And, considering how her body tingled as his gaze traveled over her, he still made her bread rise.

Ugh.

"It's a bit loud for eight p.m. on a Sunday," he added.

"It's that late?" Pity her neighbors. Most were young professionals fixing up cool old houses like she was, but some families with young children as well as a couple of seniors rallying against downsizing occupied the friendly block. "Go ahead." Hammers and screwdrivers clunking, she unhooked her tool belt and draped it over the sofa back. "And then you can explain why you entered my house without knocking."

She sounded like a hag about to cast an evil spell, but the shock of seeing Brett after all this time zapped a pang deep into her heart. He had hurt her. Badly. He couldn't waltz in here smelling like sandalwood as if nothing had ever happened and expect her to offer him tea and croissants.

He switched off the player. "I parked on the street and heard the music when I got out. I knocked, but you didn't hear me. The door was open, so I came in."

A habit formed when they were kids, with her parents' blessing.

Her face warmed. "The neighbors don't mind my music." Until dinnertime. *Ahem.* "They know what I'm doing."

"What are you doing?"

Oh, no. He didn't get to ask the questions. She hadn't heard a peep from Brett since the night she'd handed him her virginity. What a fool she'd been, fancying herself in love with the guy, trusting him to help her over the hurdle of the Big V. Anticipating he would call or text or *somehow* stay in touch with her following her brother's wedding. To cradle her until the soft light of dawn washed the hotel room hadn't seemed unreasonable either. Anything other than his mortifying pronouncement about how the moment she'd looked forward to for years had been 'a mistake.'

She arched her eyebrows. "Why are you here?"

He looked around, palms upturned and forehead furrowing. Flummoxed as a flea-bitten ferret.

Tori snapped her fingers. "Beep, beep, Brett. Keep up. If you're looking for Ryan, you're out of luck. He doesn't live here anymore."

The furrows deepened. "I didn't know Ry lived here."

"He needed someplace to stay when Giselle kicked him out."

Brett pushed his hands into his pants pockets. More interesting creases developed. "Yeah, Ry mentioned the divorce. She really blindsided him, huh? How is he?"

"Lousy. He needed to get away. He's scuba diving—"

"Ry?"

"—in Micronesia. He won't be back until July." Ryan needed to concentrate on himself right now, not worry about nomadic pals like Brett the Rat Bastard Evans.

The golden-haired RB frowned. "I wanted to catch up with him while I'm here. Did he say I was coming?"

"Nope. He's gone off-grid, so I can't check with him either." Tori retrieved her cell from the music dock and scanned her messages. Nothing from her helper Mick. That was odd. The nineteen-year-old was super-glued to his phone. She flicked a glance to Brett. "Don't you need to fly off somewhere?" No worries about getting cleaned up for the long haul. Leaving was Brett's specialty.

A stunned glaze slid over his face. "Tori, I just flew *here*."

Lordy-Lou, the man was unforthcoming. Lines of tiredness fanned from his eyes and mouth. Tori's chest ached. And her frustration soared.

Why should she care about the state of his health? Her tingly reaction upon seeing him again was only shock. It would wear off. Just like her heartache had.

She was over Brett Evans. Completely. Kaput. After his rejection, she'd worked hard to convince herself she wasn't coated in hot-guy repellant. She'd had relationships—one lasting a year. None had worked out the way she'd hoped, but that didn't have anything to do with Brett. Her dream man simply hadn't happened along. Yet. Tori was patient. She could wait.

"Yes, you are here," she agreed. A few screws short of a blister pack, it appeared, but an optimist might say he hovered in the vicinity of 'present.' "Did you come to Portland for one of your software thingies?"

He nodded. "Where are your parents? Will they be home later?"

He flashed the same wide grin employed countless times when they were teenagers. Her tummy swooped.

Careful, she instructed her soft heart. The Evans charm was lethal. She would not succumb. But she wasn't above torturing the man who'd caused her several tear-filled nights.

"Let me think." She touched a finger to pursed lips. "It's June in two days, so they're in North—no, South Dakota. Visiting Mount Rushmore, checking out giant president heads."

Brett pulled one hand out of his pants pockets. His fingers flexed. "When will they return?"

"In September." The faint echo of Rex's baying carried from the backyard. Tori cocked an ear. If she didn't bring in her dog soon, her neighbors would complain—and not about the music.

"You're renovating their house while they're gone?"

"Ohhh." Now she knew what twisted Brett's boxer-briefs. Ry hadn't told him she'd bought their parents' house. "No, I'm working on my house." Phone tucked in a palm, she crossed her arms. "Mom and Dad sold me the place. They're touring the country on twin Harleys."

"You're kidding." A corner of Brett's mouth tipped up. "I can't picture your mom riding a Hog."

"They love it. Dad sold the hardware store to a chain, and I'm in charge of Jarrett's now." Her mom's old video store, which had fallen on hard times as the industry crumbled. The rental library remained a hit with enthusiasts who valued personal recommendations and titles difficult to find online, as well as with older folks unaccustomed to streaming. The rest of the store was a work in progress. "They're moving into a gated community in the fall. Most of their furniture is in storage, except for the pieces they gave me."

"Well, that changes things."

"For you, maybe." Rex's howling grew louder. Tori glanced over her shoulder. "Excuse me." Clutching her cell, she arrowed for the kitchen.

Brett stared at the swinging door leading to the rear of the Jarretts'—correction—Tori's house. Had she *dismissed* him? Was he supposed to swivel around on his wingtips and leave?

He wiped his mouth. Man, he'd screwed up. Again. He'd thought he had his month in Portland mapped out. He would settle in with Tori's folks, enjoy some beers with Ryan, begin his consulting assignment, then formulate a plan for talking to Tori.

Face to face. Not through email or texting or the facade of social media.

Damn it, he'd *known* he should have resisted their attraction during those weeks preceding Ryan's wedding. Compartmentalizing his life created the least havoc.

Havoc equaled messy. Messy morphed into complicated. Complicated set off emotional explosions, the very aspect of human existence Brett sought to avoid.

But come on! Tori's flirting at the couples shower, the sizzling glances she'd sent his way during the rehearsal dinner, and their passionate kisses on the ballroom balcony at the tail end of the reception had conspired against his best intentions—yes, his level best—never to show interest in Ryan Jarrett's sister.

"It's okay, Brett," she'd whispered in his ear on that private balcony...in the elevator...as they hurried down the corridor to his hotel room. *"I want you, Brett. Say you want me too."*

Of course, he'd wanted her. Slush didn't move through his veins.

That didn't change the glaring fact that he'd *known* he was eighty types of wrong for a marriage-oriented woman like Tori Jarrett, but he'd tumbled into bed with her anyway.

The topper? He'd discovered her virginal status...a few inches too late. Bringing sex into their relationship had ruined everything.

Steeling himself, he entered the kitchen as a young beagle raced in from the back porch. The dog pounced on a bowl brimming with kibbles and gobbled the food.

Tori closed the door with a resounding thump. "You're still here?"

"Yep." They both had some explaining to do.

"Why? Brett, I'm tired—" The landline on the counter rang, cutting her off. Plunking down her cell, she checked the machine's display. "That might be Mick."

"Who?"

"A college kid from the neighborhood. He's helping with the house renovations."

Brett's jaw ticked. "I'll wait."

Rolling her eyes, she answered the phone. While she spoke to the Mick dude, Brett glanced around the kitchen that had felt more like home to him growing up than his own mother's kitchen. As much as he loved his mom and appreciated the difficulties of a divorced woman raising a child alone, nothing replaced the feeling of being part of a real family. He'd found that with the Jarretts.

"Hey, Mick, how are you?" Tori said into the receiver. "Why didn't you text or call my cell?…Yeah, it's lucky our parents both have landlines. I'll check the couch cushions for your phone…Oh, I hear you. Dead batteries suck." Her hazel eyes widened. "A broken collarbone? Mick, I'm sorry! I should have driven you to the hospital—"

The guy must have interrupted, because Tori listened intently. Her mouth twitched into a smile, and she laughed. "I hope wearing a sling doesn't chase away *all* your girlfriends. Look at it this way—maybe they'll fight over the chance to nurse you back to health."

One eye on the star-spangled roosters lining the wallpaper, Brett studied Tori discreetly. Her loose T-shirt didn't do a very effective job of disguising her breasts. If anything, they appeared fuller than he remembered. She'd lost weight in her face, emphasizing her perky nose and saucy lips. Not one dab of makeup marred her skin. Wholesome, fresh, and appealing—that was Tori Jarrett. The girl he'd grown up with and then used in the worst possible way.

"I'll reimburse the medical expenses," Tori said into the phone. "Mick, I insist. Is there anything else you need?" She laughed again. "Anything but that." Her gaze swung Brett's direction. She raised a finger, as if to indicate the call would end soon. "Are you home tomorrow?…I'll drop off your phone after work. Then I can check on you myself…Thanks, but I'll leave the drooling to your girlfriends…You too, Mick. Have a good night."

She hung up with a sigh. Her dog finished wolfing kibbles and glanced at her with bright brown eyes. She sat at the built-in breakfast nook. Leaning down and clapping her hands, she called softly, "Here, Rex."

So, Rex was the name of her dog, not a boyfriend. A restriction in Brett's chest eased as the beagle wandered over and inspected his ankles before scampering to Tori.

She rubbed her pet's floppy ears.

"How's your friend?" Brett dipped his head in an attempt to catch her gaze. "A broken collarbone doesn't sound fun." From what he'd gathered of the phone call, this Mick bozo had fallen off the stepladder and busted his clavicle. The dope's head must have been anywhere but on the responsibility of helping Tori.

Her lips twisted. "It's a small fracture, but he needs to wear a sling. He can't work on the living room anymore. That's not my concern, but it was nice to have his help."

"How did he fall?" The ladder measured five feet.

"I have no clue. My back was turned. Mick's in pain, so I won't quiz him." Tori fondled her dog's ears again. Issuing a contented canine moan, Rex stretched his muzzle until she included the animal's chin and throat in the gentle massage.

Lucky beast.

"Why do you care, Brett? Do you even remember Mick?"

Brett shook his head to clear sudden images of Tori's supple hands on his hardening body, her fingers touching and stroking. He was clearly out of line. Way out.

"No," he said evenly. "Should I?"

"His mom was Mrs. Turner around the corner. Mick took his stepfather's surname when she remarried. He's Mick Seifert these days."

"Oh, him. He went by Mikey then." A real hell-raiser, if Brett remembered correctly, and, judging from Tori's side of their conversation, currently a dumbass pervert in need of butt-kicking, college student or not.

Tori waved a hand. "Let's return to why you're here."

"I wanted to discuss that ten minutes ago."

"And *I* want to discuss it now."

Brett bit back a retort. If he had learned anything as a child of a rocky marriage, it was that arguing rarely solved anything. Rational conversation was the key.

"What's eating you?" he asked in a benign tone.

"Nothing." She stroked her panting dog until the animal curled beneath the table.

"Tori, something is bugging you—"

Her chin tucked in. "I'm not upset."

"You're angry."

"No, I'm not."

Brett smiled. "Really? Then why does that tiny groove between your eyebrows remind me of when Ry and I stole your favorite dress-up doll? The cutie with the baseball uniform and miniature glove. You were one ticked-off nine-year-old when you couldn't find her to take to your Little League game. You gave me lip for days."

Cheeks blazing tomato-red, she jumped off the cushioned seat and swept past him to the refrigerator. The subtle scent of her work-earned perspiration emanated from her glowing skin as she hauled out a bottle of chilled water.

"Brett." She uncapped the bottle and drank, hand jerking. A tiny splash of liquid splattered the linoleum. "Why are you hanging around? You must have picked up by now that you're not welcome."

Major miscalculation with the Little League reference. Throat drying, he spread his hands. "Just sorting things out. You see, Ry arranged for me to rent a room from your parents. Here. In the house I thought they owned. I was more than happy to take the reins, but he offered to talk to them. I was neck-deep in work, so I agreed."

"Humph." Her ponytail swung back and forth. "It never occurred to you to confirm before showing up?"

"I tried." The *Keep Portland Weird* stitching decorating her ball cap loomed like a doomsday warning. "I left two messages on the answering machine last week." He pointed at the obsolete contraption on the counter. "Your mom's voice is still on the recording, by the way."

Tori scratched her neck. "Yeah. I...um...left it on there to help finalize some things for Dad. They're transferring the number to their new address in the fall. It seemed the easiest solution for everyone."

"Did you receive my messages?"

She examined her fingernails.

"Tori?"

"I got them. But as soon as I heard you say, *'Hi, Marty and Linda, it's Brett Evans,'* I deleted them." She beamed a completely unrepentant smile.

"What are you saying? Did Ry arrange for me to rent a room or not?"

"I doubt it. When did you and he last talk?"

"Three months ago. I was in Dallas, so we texted."

"There you go." Tori drank her water. "My parents did own the house then. Ry stayed with them until he left."

Brett ruminated over this mystifying new scrap of information. He'd completed his last software optimization gig on Friday, sixteen-hundred miles away in Omaha. Three weeks of untangling the bugs in an aerospace company's computer systems had just about crossed his eyes. The spring schedule he'd accepted with his employer, DataPrimer, Inc., had allowed him thirty hours at his Sacramento apartment before he'd needed to fly to Portland today, and exhaustion fogged his brain.

Had he misinterpreted his text exchange with Ryan? How deep a hole had he dug himself?

"I don't get it," he appealed to Tori's customary good nature. "If Ry was having that rough a time, why offer to speak to your folks on my behalf?"

"Because"—she adjusted the bill of her baseball cap with a sharp tug—"that's Ryan. Always trying to be a good guy. Giselle flattened him. Like a pizza. *Capiche?* He could barely think straight. He didn't intend to forget whatever you and he discussed. Sheesh."

"All right, all right." Brett gestured at her water bottle. "Do you have a spare?"

"Knock yourself out." She sidestepped him as he reached for the fridge handle. Their arms brushed, and the brief contact zinged him to the bone.

"However," she continued, "if Ryan had said anything about you renting a room, Mom and Dad would have told me when I bought the house. That was five weeks ago, and they didn't breathe a word."

"Perfect," Brett mumbled with a touch of sarcasm. Another stretch of impersonal housekeeping services and high-calorie restaurant food awaited him. Whatever hotel he might locate at this late hour better have a well-equipped gym. "Any chance you'd honor Ry's arrangements?"

Tori's eyes hurled thunderbolts into his skull. "And let *you* stay *here* where *I* live? Are you nuts?"

"Relax. I'm joking." He was now. "I'm here for a month, Tori. I was looking forward to a break from hotel living, that's all." He twisted the cap off his water bottle.

"Then maybe a career change is in order."

He set his bottle on the counter without drinking. "Is this about us having sex?"

She flinched. "Oh, you have some nerve showing your face around here and asking about texting arrangements with Ry after your big 'mistake' with me!" Water flipped out of her bottle as she air-quoted, and the liquid dampened her T-shirt. "Of course it's about us having sex!" Her dog whimpered beneath the table. She turned. "Shh, Rex, it's okay," she soothed the dog in a lullaby tone. Then, slowly, her gaze resettled on Brett. "I was a twenty-two-year-old virgin, Brett. You slept with me and then skipped town. Let that sink in for a second."

Brett's pulse accelerated. "Now, Tori, you say it like I left Portland because we slept together. That's not what happened. I was moving anyway."

"In six weeks!" Her hands flung out—and water arced onto his shirt this time. Wet fabric plastered his hot skin. "Deflowering me made you run away to Sacramento that night!"

"Tori, we talked about this then."

"No, you talked. You so clearly wanted to get away from me, I wasn't about to stop you. Do you have any idea how humiliated I felt?" Pain shone in her eyes and radiated from her rigid stance.

Damn it, damn it, damn it. He had hurt her far more than he'd realized. More than she had let on. But when had he allowed her the opportunity to tell him?

He needed her to understand. "Yes, I left, and...I know it sounds bad that I didn't make it to the present-opening barbecue the next day. When I checked my phone that night"—in the hotel corridor, after she'd booted him out of his hotel room—"I realized DataPrimer left a message during the ceremony, while my cell was off. There was an urgent contract with a major client, and they needed extra hands on-site. I thought—well, you and I—I thought a clean break was best, and I wanted to make a good impression on my boss..." He winced. That sounded so lame.

She snarled, "You wanted? To make? A good? Impression?" She threw the remainder of her water in his face. "Up yours, Brett Hennessy Evans!"

"Okay, I earned that," he blubbered through the chilly liquid dribbling off his lips.

"You earned this too." She grabbed his full bottle off the counter and sloshed icy water onto his pants zipper.

His genitals shriveled. Rex popped up from beneath the nook table, trotted to Brett's shoes, and slurped the liquid pooling on the kitchen floor.

Brett stood there, drenched from chin to crotch. This conversation wasn't going anything like he'd imagined. Tori wasn't usually a drama queen—which meant he was king of the idiots, past, present, and well into the future.

"Tori," he murmured, moving toward her. "I'm sorry."

Her hands trembled on the bottles gripped gunslinger-style at her hips. "I know you are." The bottles jiggled, and her trigger fingers bounced. "That's the most frustrating part of this whole embarrassing episode. Evans, for a smart guy, you're clueless."

A bit of water dribbled from one container, splashing her sneakers. She eyed the remaining liquid in the bottle.

Brett didn't budge. If it helped her feel better, she could construct a dam and surge the Willamette River his way.

Tori downed the water and lobbed both empties into the sink.

Brett's breath whistled out from between his teeth. "Let me make it up to you. Can't we—"

"You haven't contacted me since that night." Her chin lifted. "We had a lot of fun in the weeks before the wedding. You sniffed around me throughout the reception."

"That's not quite how I remember it."

"*You*. Sniffed around. *Me*. I encouraged you, but *you* did not discourage me."

"I was an ass," Brett admitted as her dog snuffled his sodden wingtips. "I'm older now. Wiser."

She snorted.

He looked out the window. "Tori, I don't want to fight with you. Before that night, I thought of you as the kid sister I'd never had."

"You'd sleep with your kid sister?"

"You know what I mean." He met her gaze. "Our childhood means something to me, and I didn't—don't—want to lose it. If I'd stuck around until my original moving date…" How could he have resisted her, having become well acquainted by then with how warm and willing and loving and caring she was? He would have wanted her over and over. To no good end. "If I'd stayed, I would have hurt you more than I did by ripping off the bandage and leaving then," he said quietly.

She scoffed. "Ego much? Maybe I only wanted one night, to get rid of my virginity with a guy I thought I could trust."

"If that were true, you would have mentioned your...limited experience before we went upstairs."

Her face reddened. "If I'd *said* I'd only had battery-operated lovers until you, you wouldn't have slept with me!"

Bingo. He wouldn't have.

He shouldn't have hooked up with her regardless.

"We can debate the issue until your parents return. The point is, if I'd stayed, emotions might have escalated." Her eyes narrowed to slits, and his heart thudded. "Nothing positive would have come out of me leaving six weeks into a relationship. Tori, I would have lost the you I've always known, one of my few childhood buddies." Apparently, he'd lost her anyway. Worse, until tonight, he hadn't fully realized it. He softened his tone. "You know, we could approach my stay in town as a chance to work on our friendship."

The look she gave him could have clipped his toenails. "That's not gonna happen." She grabbed a soda from the fridge. "Come on, Rex." The dog's ears pricked. "You can nap on my bed while I take a shower. Then we'll make popcorn with loads of salt and butter and watch violent movies in my room. Sounds therapeutic." Her gaze flew to Brett. "You know your way out. Don't worry about the door. I'll lock it."

2

$\mathcal{B}$RETT PARKED HIS rental car in the alley behind Tori's house and tossed his sunglasses onto the passenger seat. Squinting against the bright noon sunshine, he climbed out of the sedan and unlatched the gate in the white picket fence. The new work pants he'd changed into an hour ago felt stiff around the knees. Tackling Tori's renovations would break in the jeans—provided she wasn't hanging around the place to derail his plans and send him packing again.

Yesterday, after she ordered him gone, he'd paced his motel room, wondering how to atone for having hurt her so badly. The answer had whacked him like a sack of nails. Every woman he'd dated had appreciated his handyman skills, learned from Marty Jarrett while palling around with Ryan. Tori possessed toned muscle along with her luscious curves, but Brett hit the gym on a regular basis and could power through heavy jobs in half the time.

He stole through the tree-shaded yard, sneakers quiet on the grass. No deafening music thundered from the house. And Tori's dog appeared nowhere in sight.

Excellent. Last night, while Tori spoke to Mick Seifert, she'd mentioned dropping in after work today to return the dope's cell phone. That must be where she was. Or at her store, now dubbed the Retro Vibe. Brett had communicated with Ryan enough over the years to keep tabs on Tori's efforts helping her mom navigate Jarrett's Video through various incarnations when digital streaming nearly decimated the family's second business. Some googling this morning revealed the shop had expanded to include selling new vinyl records as well as refurbished and replica hi-fis. The website featured a news clip showcasing Tori and her mom discussing the resurgence in the popularity of LPs among millennials and music buffs. In the clip, Linda Jarrett said capitalizing on the revitalization of vinyl as a way to modernize the store while retaining a large catalogue of movies had been Tori's brainwave. Pretty damn impressive.

Patting the pocket of his flannel shirt stuffed with dog treats, Brett crept onto the back porch. Rex's head pushed through a pet flap in the kitchen door. Seemed Tori had left the flap open so the dog could access the yard in her absence. Yesterday, a plastic overlay had sealed shut the route.

"Hey, boy." Brett crouched and offered two treats from his palm. Rex scrambled onto the porch and devoured the bribe. Brett chuckled. "You're easy to please, aren't you, buddy?" Rex whined and pawed Brett's thigh. "More treats later, boy. We have work to do."

Standing, Brett rapped on the door. "Hmm." He looked at Rex. "I don't hear a thing. Is Tori at the store?"

The dog's head tilted, a brown ear sliding to cover one eye.

"She's either at the store or nursing busted eardrums."

Rex's mouth hung open as the animal panted.

"You're right," Brett responded. "She might be wearing music buds and meditating on a magic carpet for all I know. I'll just have to risk it." He tested the doorknob. Locked.

Smiling, he slid his fingers into a jeans pocket and retrieved the old house key he'd brought from California to save the Jarretts the hassle of cutting another. He waggled the key at Rex. "Cross your whiskers this thing works, boy, because I doubt I could squeeze through your doggy door." And if Tori or her parents had installed an alarm, police sirens hello.

Brett slipped the key into the lock. It fit—and no clanging alarm. His smile broadened.

Entering the house with Rex on his heels, he called into the quiet. "Tori?" His voice echoed off the walls. "So far so good."

A portable pet fence blocked the swinging door at the far right of the kitchen. On the left, the open entry to Tori's childhood bedroom drew Brett's gaze to a closed, additional exit to the hallway which, when ajar, provided access to the shared main-floor bathroom and master bedroom. Tori's dog became Brett's best friend as Brett poked his head into the small second bedroom. Tori had made good use of the quirky architectural feature of the extra door. Between installing the pet gate in the kitchen and shutting this access to the hall, she'd protected her dog from renovation dangers at the front of the house.

A mussed blanket covered the foot of the narrow bed. Rex's napping spot?

Brett stared at the lone pillow. Did Tori sleep in here at night or in a larger bed in the master bedroom? His jeans zipper tightened.

He retreated to the kitchen, Rex following. A slip of notepaper beckoned from the breakfast table. Crossing the room, Brett scanned a to-do list complete with doodles and color-coded ink. Typical cheerful, organized Tori.

He tapped the list. "Lookee here, Rex. She even left instructions." It must be fate.

Tori might hate him now, but redemption would be his the moment she came home.

❧

Bath. Bed. Walk Rex.

Yawning, Tori locked her bike and helmet to the rack under the eaves at the outside corner of her old room. "Amendment," she muttered, feeling addle-brained. "First walk Rex, then bed." She shook her head. "No, then bath." Still not right. "Walk Rex then eat. *Then* bath and bed."

Rex. Eat. Bath. Bed. R-E-B-B. REBB. She could remember that, couldn't she?

Stepping onto the porch, she rummaged through her back-pack-style purse for her house keys. She shoved the key into the lock.

Icy tentacles skittered along her spine.

The mechanism moved far too easily. Which meant the door wasn't locked. Brett's guerilla assault on her peace of mind had shadowed her restless sleep until three a.m., but only an airhead left her doors unlocked two days in a row.

Carefully withdrawing the key, she glanced down.

Rex hadn't raced out of his doggy door to greet her the instant she'd planted her foot on the porch. Not only that, but no paw prints marked the painted wood or beagle-themed welcome mat.

Her dog ran in and out of the house several times a day, yet no grassy bits or clods of earth or dandelion roots or remnants of other Rexxy hobbies littered the area. Eerily, the area surrounding the mat appeared wiped clean.

Tori's fingers shook. Oh, Lord. Had someone broken into her house and hurt Rex? She'd adopted him from her parents when she bought the place but already thought of him as her little guy. She loved the inquisitive nose-on-legs. She would never forgive herself if he lay injured in a ditch, had been shaved by a Satanic cult, or been sold because of his pedigree. Or, heaven forbid, held for ransom!

A Christopher Walken film from last night's marathon cast an evil light on that very topic. If some creep had nabbed her dog—

Heart thumping, she raced to the window of her old room and plastered her palms against the glass, eyes peeled as she peered between the blinds. Rex slept on her old twin bed, legs and saggy lips twitching.

She hadn't locked the door! What a no-mind. She was totally losing it.

No more psychopath movies. She was cut off.

Pulse settling, she entered the kitchen and plopped her purse on the counter. "Here, Rex."

Her pet's sleepy rustlings carried from the open bedroom. Claws clicked on hardwood as he lumbered off the bed and trundled into the kitchen. He downward-dogged onto his short forelegs.

"Hi, sweetie." Tori knelt on the linoleum and scratched his muzzle. "Aw, you're worn out. Busy chasing butterflies today? How about a treat and walk?"

Rex perked up at *treat* and *walk*. He trotted to the breakfast nook and sniffed the air.

Tori glanced over, brow wrinkling and nostrils tickling as she caught the scent enchanting her hound. The pet gate leaned against a cupboard, while plates, cutlery, glasses, and a bucket of fried chicken adorned the turquoise Formica table.

An image of the suspiciously clean back porch popped to mind. What was this—a warped version of Goldilocks visiting the three bears?

She fumed. No self-respecting criminal would case the joint and then provide dinner. Goldi-his-head-was-about-to-be-crammed-into-a-blender was more like it!

From deep within the house, the toilet flushed. Tori folded her arms as Brett the Golden-Haired Rat Bastard Evans shouldered open the swinging door and sauntered into the kitchen.

"Hey, Rex, time to—" Brett froze, gaze widening as Tori glared machetes at him. Rex scampered to the man and pawed his leg. A fake innocent smile spread over Brett's face. "Hi, Tori."

Her jaw stiffened. Any guilt she'd experienced over forcing him to find a hotel last night—and she'd only felt a *pinch* of guilt —promptly vanished. He had broken into her house and bewitched her dog, deep-fried-chickened her kitchen, and mopped her back porch. This wasn't a warped version of Goldilocks, but a mutation of Snow White. And, oh, boy, did she have a poisoned apple for him.

She jammed her hands on her hips. "Don't 'Hi, Tori' me, Brett Evans. What the bleep are you doing?"

His eyebrows vaulted into his hairline. "The bleep?"

"The bleep, the blap, the flipping frack." She tried not to swear around Rex. Dogs were sensitive creatures.

"That clears it up. And I'm glad you asked because there's something I want to—"

"*Brett,*" she interrupted, in no mood for fending off his legendary charm. Who cared if her PMS-ravaged body craved the aromatic scent of a dozen different herbs and spices wafting from the chicken bucket? If Brett thought comfort food would salvage the atrocity of breaking into her house, he was bleeping, blapping mistaken. "What part of 'leave now' did you not understand last night?"

His gaze darted back and forth. "Technically, you didn't say, 'Leave now.' You said, 'You know your way out.' As it happens, I also know my way back in." He placed a key on the nook table.

"Is that my hidie key?" How dare he scrounge in her cute flowerbeds for the clever fake rock!

He shook his head. "Your mom gave me a copy when I was thirteen. You can have it back. I only needed it today."

Tori couldn't fathom why he'd kept a key to the house for seventeen years. It was difficult enough coming to grips with the sight of him in low-riding jeans and a blue-checkered work shirt with rolled-up sleeves accentuating his corded forearms. What kind of company did he consult for? Hotties R Us?

"Why did you mop my back porch?" Flint chipped off her voice.

"I dirtied it carrying the paneling to the garage."

"You carried the paneling to the garage?"

"Yeah," Brett replied as Rex leapt against the table and strained to paw the chicken bucket. Brett ordered the dog to sit. Like that was gonna happen. Beagles sat when it suited them, unless a person dangled food in front of their eager black noses. Brett added a simple hand gesture, and Tori's little hound sat.

What?

"You had 'Call Marlow's about paneling' written on your to-do list," Brett said in an irritatingly reasonable tone. "I googled the place. Turns out they resell salvage from renovation sites."

He could maybe tell her something she didn't know.

"They'll pick up the paneling tomorrow. The sheets are leaning against the garage, covered with a tarp. Didn't you see them?"

"No." She'd entered the yard from the side gate today, not the alley. "I worried someone broke into the house. I thought they might have hurt Rex."

Air whistled through Brett's teeth. "Didn't think about that. Bad timing with me visiting the can just now. I planned to wait for you on the porch. Rex and I wanted to surprise you."

Her dog wanted to surprise her? "By arranging to have the paneling picked up before I took down every sheet? Thanks a lot, Brett. Now I'll have to work all night to finish the job." Her voice grated in her throat, and she hated every whiny, complaining note shattering her ears. She wasn't this person. She wasn't ornery Tori. She was friendly, happy, big-hearted Tori.

Everybody said so! Everyone loved her!

The older and supposedly wiser Brett Hennessy Evans sucking up all the molecules in her too-warm kitchen pushed buttons she hadn't realized she possessed. If she let down her guard around this man, she could rapidly find herself in serious trouble. She'd crushed on Brett from the time she was ten until he'd karate-chopped her heart into dry bits of clay at her brother's wedding.

He hadn't once returned her feelings. Was she incapable of learning her lesson with this guy?

"Don't stress about the paneling," he said. "I removed it. The living room, the dining room, and the hall, like your errand list said."

She wanted to cry. "You did all that work? Why?"

"Because. After I found a place to crash, I started thinking." His deep voice gentled. "I behaved horribly the night of Ry and Giselle's wedding. I acted like my dad, Tori,"—a grimace pulled down his lips—"not considering how my actions affected the people I care about. Realizing that disgusted me. Seeing you again yesterday and really understanding the hell I put you through sickens me more. Ripping off the bandage and skipping town, as you so aptly put it, might have worked for me four years ago, but it did bupkis for you. I'm not trying to make excuses, but after I moved to Sacramento, I got dragged into the never-ending whirl-wind of consulting gigs. My schedule is crazy, and that's my doing, my responsibility. I lost contact with so many old friends, I can't tell you. Tori...that's how I need to think of you now. As a friend."

She chewed the inside of her cheek. *Great*. One step up from kid sister.

"Granted, I haven't been a very good friend. I can fix that now. What I did today was a peace offering." He reached out a hand. "Let me show you."

Trying to absorb the enormity of everything he'd said, she did what she had promised herself she would never do again. She went to him.

His hand curled around her upper arm, his palm warm on her skin. The old, familiar heat swam within her. She wore jeans and her cobalt-blue Retro Vibe polo shirt, and it occurred to her the shade coordinated perfectly with his checkered flannel.

To look at them, they matched. On the outside. Inside, where it mattered, they wanted opposite things out of life. They always had.

"Didn't you work today?" she asked, as he steered her toward the living room.

"My contract starts tomorrow. June first. I had free time. A rarity these days."

"What about the hotel? Where are you staying?"

"The Rosebud yesterday and again tonight." He named an economy motel not far from the store. "Beginning tomorrow, I booked a hotel close to Sugartree Electric, where I'm consulting. It's nice, but this weekend a room is coming available at a suite hotel in the same area. They have mini-kitchens and a better gym. I'll move for the last time Saturday."

She didn't feel guilty about the hotel swaps. Uh-uh. Nope. Not a bit.

"Let's have some fun," he said. "Close your eyes."

She cooperated but not because he asked. Rather because she didn't want anything resembling guilt emanating from her gaze.

"Can we make this quick? I need to walk Rex."

"Already done."

"What?" Her eyes winged open. Brett's hand slid over her face to close them again...and stayed there. Her lashes feathered against his palm.

"Tut-tut." His low voice raced jittery sensations throughout her body. "He became restless around two. We played tug-a-stick out back, but your dog has energy to spare. I hitched him to his leash and headed to the playing fields where Ry and I goofed around in high school. The skate park is a nice addition."

Tori's fingers splayed. "You can't walk him in the skateboard park. The sign says No Dogs. What if he left a land mine?"

"I noticed compostable pet bags in the same drawer as the

leash. I took one along. Once I saw the bylaw sign, I asked around and located the dog park. Rex sniffed some buddies."

Yes, her pet had quite the assortment of human and canine friends. "Where's the bag now?" Translation: *Did you use it?*

"In your outside trashcan." Code Deciphered: *Yep.*

"Do you have a dog in California?" Tori asked as Brett's hand shifted on her face, allowing light to sliver through his fingers.

"With my schedule? Not a chance. Why?"

"No reason," Tori replied while they inched toward the swinging door. Brett handled Rex like he was born to it, despite that he'd hadn't owned a dog as a child—or at any other time, apparently. His parents divorced when he was six, and his dad hadn't remained in Portland long. His mom, a practical nurse, had picked up overtime whenever possible. The woman's twelve-hour shifts had ruled out dogs and she was allergic to cats.

When Tori was five and Brett nine, Sharon Evans brought home a rabbit for her son. The kind woman sneezed for days, her eyes growing red and swollen. Returning the bunny to the pet store had seemed the only option, until Tori's parents caved to her pleas to let Bungee live with them. Brett visited the bunny often, and Tori smothered the tiny animal with affection.

Then Bungee fell sick and died. Brett, Tori, and Ryan held a somber memorial service between two rose bushes in Tori's mother's back garden. Tori would never forget Brett drying her tears with his scraggly cartoon-character T-shirt. She had nurtured a soft spot for him since.

That damn spot. Her lips curled. Why had he needed to treat her so *decently*? Two years later, he stood up for her against a crew of seventh-grade boys teasing her for being a shrimp, and her on-again-off-again crush had sparkled to life. Her young heart hadn't stood a chance.

"Make sure Rex comes with us, so he doesn't steal the chicken," she mumbled as they proceeded into the living room.

Brett's hand stayed over her eyes, and his chuckle warmed her deep inside. "Hungry?"

"No." Her stomach grumbled. "If Rex has a chance to steal food, he will. He thinks my dad is his alpha male. I need to train him to obey me."

"That's why he likes me. I'm pure alpha."

Tori's mouth quirked. "Don't flatter yourself."

His grip remained firm on her arm. "Come, Rex," he called.

The pad of Brett's empty ring finger bumped Tori's nose as her dog trundled alongside them, nasal passages snuffling the carpet.

The door whisked shut.

Brett's hands lowered from her face.

Tori gawked. "Oh, my God." He had removed every sheet of painted paneling, revealing old wiring and the insulation previous owners had installed while updating the original plaster walls. Hearing Brett had accomplished hours of work was one thing, seeing the evidence quite another. This morning, dust and wood shavings had littered a small number of exposed cross-studs. Now, the skeleton walls were vacuumed clean. The shop vacuum hunched near the fireplace, and Tori's hand tools and Rex's chew toy lay inches from the hearth. Casting a glance to the corridor and open master bedroom, she spotted more bare studs. "This would have taken me another three days."

Brett flexed a bicep. "They didn't give us alpha males sheer brutish strength for nothing."

She barely succeeded in restraining a smile. Rex danced around Brett's shins, and she glared at her dog. *Traitor.*

Her gaze rested on the empty area beneath the picture window. "Uh, Brett, where are my baseboards and crown moldings? They're original—1931. I wanted to sand and refinish them."

A smile brightened his handsome face. "Your note said 'Remove nails from baseboards' and 'Buy stain.' I completed the first task."

"You removed those horrible nails?" Eighty-year-old oak moldings were thick and dense, much sturdier than contemporary baseboard and crown. Extracting the entrenched spikes murdered her shoulders.

Brett nodded. "I stashed everything in your dad's old workshop downstairs. I noticed a couple of vintage hi-fis in there. Are they for your store?"

"Yeah. Refinishing them is Dad's retirement project."

"It's a great idea, for the store and your dad. He's not the type to loaf around. By the way"—Brett patted her wrist—"I saw Ry's weights and treadmill in the rec room. Or are they yours?"

"They're Ryan's." But why mention the exercise equipment? She lifted her hands. "Brett, I hope you don't think doing all this work means you can stay here now."

He stepped back. "Why would I think that?"

"I don't know. Why would you spend your free day handy-manning my house?"

"Tori, I told you. It's an olive branch."

Rex pranced to the chew toy, trapped the stuffed fox beneath a paw, and gnawed an ear.

"And you honestly don't expect anything in return?"

Brett smiled like a beatific pontiff addressing a crowd. "I do want something."

She knew it! "What?"

"I want to prove I can be a good friend. As in platonic. Sex and friendship don't mix. For you and me anyway. Before Ry and Giselle's wedding, you and I were great pals."

"*Pals?*" Every time he mentioned that night, it stung. "Gee, Evans, you weren't complaining on the dance floor." Or in his hotel room. Until the deed was accomplished, at any rate. Then he'd behaved as if she'd neglected to mention she carried the bubonic plague.

"Can you say 'extenuating circumstances?' We got carried away."

She crossed her arms. "Nope. Can't say it. That's too many syllables for me."

His blue eyes darkened to slate. "Like I was *trying* to say, some women, especially those a guy has known since she was a baby, make great pals." He gestured as if moving an object from one pile to another. "And other women make great—"

"Lays?"

"Damn it, Tori, I never said you weren't a great lay."

But she hadn't been worthy of pursuing a real relationship. She hadn't even merited one of his infamous friends-with-benefits arrangements.

"I couldn't have been that great, it being my first time," she muttered.

He paused. "I said it last night and I'll say it again, I refuse to fight with you, Tori. Your first time should have been special."

"It *was*." In the exhilarating moments prior to his *You're a virgin?* speech.

"With the right sort of man," he tacked on in a stern voice.

"You were! I thought you were."

He stared at her. "With a guy who realized what was at stake *going in*."

"'Going in.' Har-har." That night, Tori was ecstatic, high on lust and the longings of her rather naive heart, she realized in retrospect. She had waited forever for Brett to notice her, and finally he had. Not as the tomboy kid sister of his best friend. Not as the third bridesmaid in Ry and Giselle's wedding. But as *her*, the woman. *Tori*. That he might drop her like a mildewed sock seconds after sealing the deal hadn't crossed her mind.

"Believe it or not, I don't want to fight with you either, Brett." She gestured around the living room, her dog cozy beside the hearth, chewing his toy. "All this work you've done is wonderful. I can call the electrician right away. Thank you. But it can't make up for the past." Not even a start.

"It could if you would loosen up and let it."

"If I let you appease your guilty conscience, you mean."

She wasn't being fair. Their falling into bed four years ago had been just as much her responsibility. She hadn't wanted to lose the Big V to any dude. She wasn't the type to troll the clubs, pinpoint a guy, and drag him home. She had wanted Brett and only Brett. Her singlemindedness might have clouded her judgment.

But she hadn't totally lacked in experience. She'd fooled around with a couple of boyfriends in high school and practiced plenty with the battery-operated variety in an effort not to let the cat out of the bag too quickly with Brett, as it were.

Her quite-literal pains in the weeks before her brother's wedding had wound up being for naught. She'd climaxed beneath Brett's talented mouth in the huge hotel bed, the dim light of the nightstand lamp illuminating their bodies. Seconds later, he'd cradled her face and placed a tender kiss on her lips.

She had felt oh-so-ready, and he had seemed lost in her.

When they'd first rushed into the room, laughing and kissing and tearing off each other's clothes, she definitely hadn't imagined his passionate moans as she'd unzipped his tailored pants and pleasured him in a way she hadn't experienced with any guy before him.

He hadn't caught on when *he* was in her mouth. But the instant he'd slid inside her body and realized the accommodations weren't as roomy as he might have expected, a look of sheer terror had dropped over his face.

"You're a virgin?" he'd asked. The humiliating memory surged. *"Tori, why didn't you say something?"*

"It's okay, Brett. I want it to be you." She undulated her hips beneath his solid weight, and he groaned.

"It's not okay," he whispered roughly.

"Oh, yes, it is." She grabbed his butt and sank him home, wincing at the keen bite of momentary pain.

A gasp shot out of his mouth—and then he moaned. Long and low and growly, heat glazing his eyes.

Mouth on hers, hands on her breasts, he pumped slow, steady strokes until her discomfort eased. Then he plunged harder and faster, as if losing control.

"Tori, Tori." His voice burrowed inside her chest, stealing her breath.

"Yes, Brett. Please."

He slipped a hand between their writhing bodies and brought her to the precipice. She toppled over in elation.

With a final thrust, he joined her.

In college, her friends had cautioned that the first time hurt too much to truly enjoy. But Tori had done her homework, and she'd enjoyed herself to the bursting, bright, glittering stars and back.

It's him, it's him, her yearning heart had chanted.

Now, as Brett stood in her living room, arms spread and dense male confusion contorting his features, she pictured him rolling off her in the hotel bed. For the space of five heartbeats, they'd rested quietly beneath the tangled sheets. Then...

"Tori." He bent his arm on his forehead. "You should have told me."

The admonishment in his voice seared her skin. She held the sheets to her chin. "Most men would consider it an honor."

"I'm not most men." He bolted up to sit on the mattress edge. "This was a mistake."

Her heart had split into a trillion pieces. She had been so eager to show him what he was missing—what he could have —with her.

Instead of seeing the beauty in their lovemaking, he'd launched into lecture-mode about the sanctity of their childhoods, interpreting her special moment as some sort of betrayal.

Struggling not to cry, she'd yanked on her panties and locked him out of the room. *His* room. Whatever. A gentleman would have relinquished the much-needed privacy. And he had, his escaping footsteps echoing each painful beat of her heart.

The hurt she'd considered ancient history until he showed up seeking redemption sluiced through her anew, fresh and raw. She needed to protect herself. Before he hurt her again.

She tapped three fingers against her breastbone. "Sorry, Brett. I know you mean well, but I can't let you in again, not even as a friend. You can renovate the whole damn house if you want to, but I'm telling you, your convoluted strategy isn't going to work."

3

ori's Planner ~ Thought for the Day
If life gives you chicken, make chicken soup

BRETT PRIDED HIMSELF on recognizing when to back off a testy situation. He managed nicely with colleagues in a foul mood or Information Services personnel bristling against assimilating the superior DataPrimer software into their systems, often at the command of a higher-up. Sometimes he even realized when he was beat with women. And right now he was beat to a well-intentioned pulp.

Everything about Tori Jarrett—her jutting chin, her fingers jabbing her chest, the way her gaze poked barbs into his brain—brayed at him to vacate the premises and allow her to process his plea for platonic friendship in her own time.

At least, he knew where he stood with her now. In atonement limbo. She wouldn't seethe her objections if she didn't give a rip.

He lowered his hands. "All right. I hear you."

An emotion he dared not interpret flickered in her eyes. "You agree? We can't fix the past?"

"I didn't say that," he responded slowly, aware another misspoken word or phrase might incite more feminine fury. "I believe our friendship is worth salvaging, but if you don't believe it too, I won't waste your time." He'd wasted enough of the last four years. Yes, his job consumed his waking hours, but there must be more to his inexcusable behavior with Tori than work.

Once he knew a problem existed, he itched to identify and rectify it. But Tori obviously needed space.

She glanced at the carpet, curling a strand of hair behind one ear. The color, a shade darker than her luminous eyes, reminded him of sweet brown sugar.

"I appreciate everything you accomplished today," she said. "The walls. The baseboards. Walking Rex. It was a lot."

"No need to sugarcoat. I overstepped." Her response to the dismantled living room had unfolded as planned...until he'd mentioned Ryan's treadmill and weights. "I never claimed to have life figured out." Which, Brett suspected, was part of his problem. As a teenager, he'd felt like Ryan wore both shoes tied securely on his feet, whereas *he* constantly searched for a missing sneaker.

He couldn't quite put his finger on the Jarretts' magic formula for forging a strong family bond. And maybe Ryan hadn't managed to either, considering the poor guy's wife recently gave him the boot.

All Brett understood for certain was that he'd acted without honestly considering what was at stake the fateful night of Ryan's wedding. Essentially, Tori's feelings and possible dreams of a future. With him.

Months after he'd left that hotel room, the myriad ways he might have tripped up and inflicted an irreparable wound, had he stayed in Portland those additional six weeks, had haunted him. As a result, since moving to Sacramento, he had considered the consequences of his actions from every conceivable angle. To the point where he routinely banged his head against the sturdy box he had constructed for himself, as if he were a caricature of a lone-wolf road warrior aching for something indefinable. Was that any way to live?

He returned to the kitchen. Tori and Rex accompanied him.

"Where are you going?"

"To the motel. I need to review my files for Sugartree and buy dinner." The electrical manufacturing giant required hands-on training after implementation of the DataPrimer software. A monumental task.

"You can take the chicken."

He shook his head. "I brought it for you." For *them*. He had imagined the pair of them joking and laughing, sharing the meal.

Rex whined at his feet. "Hey, buddy." Brett squatted and petted the little dog's head. "We had an agreement, didn't we?" He looked up at Tori. "I promised Rex a treat this evening. I should mention he ate three throughout the day." Had he committed another gaffe, providing Rex snacks without asking Tori first?

She scratched the corner of an eye. "Which brand?"

"The lady at the pet store said these were best." He stood and withdrew the packet from his shirt pocket.

"Oh. Yeah. I guess one is fine."

The heaviness of her gaze monitored his movements as Brett fed the dog the crunchy tidbit. Rex nosed his hand. "Sorry, boy. Tori is in charge of the rest." He placed the treat packet on the counter. "These are for Rex." He withdrew his wallet from a back jeans pocket and selected a business card. Glancing around, he spotted an oversized ceramic mug stuffed with pens. He chose one and scribbled the names of the two hotels on the card. "And this is for you. Like I said, I'll move to the last place Saturday." He slid the card onto the counter and tucked his wallet into his pocket again.

Tori looked at the card but didn't touch it.

"My cell number and email address are on there." He felt like he was talking to a wall. "If you change your mind about seeing if we can become friends again, you know where to reach me."

The thought of returning to his run-down motel room bunched granite boulders between his shoulder blades. After he initiated the Sugartree contract, he'd have to look up his other old friends. His month in Portland didn't need to revolve around making things right with Tori. But, hell, he *wanted* it to.

She shook her head. "I won't need it."

"Hm? Oh, the business card." Good, she hadn't lost the ability to speak. Only the willingness to forgive. "You never know. Unless you have some other Mick to help—"

"I have loads of friends. It's not your problem."

"Well, if you need anything—a dog-walker, a drywall guy—as long as it's after five, I'm available."

Her lips thinned. His mind filled with memories of how they had felt against his own. Soft and pliant. Generous, needy, and wanting.

Damn it, he didn't *want* sexy memories of Tori. He needed her safe and secure in his heart, an anchor to happy childhood days.

No wonder he aggravated her. He aggravated *himself*.

Retrieving his rental car fob from a wall hook, he strode to the porch door.

"You forgot the chicken." Her voice sounded small.

Brett looked over his shoulder. He wanted her back in his life but not this bewildering version. No, he wanted the girl he'd once known. The woman who had listened with an open mind and an open heart. *This* Tori might as well sprout feathers and a wattle and start clucking.

"Keep it. You'll make great company for each other."

He left without explaining himself. She could chew on that particular drumstick on her own.

❦

Behind the cobalt-blue counter, Tori tracked an LP shipment on her tablet. The clickety-clack of fingernails sounded on computer keys as Meridy Ashworth, her best friend and employee, updated the Retro Vibe's social media profiles.

Meridy nudged her in the ribs. "Why so glum, Tori?"

Tori noted delivery dates. "I'm not glum. I have a lot on my mind."

"Like what? You've been quiet for hours."

"Don't be silly. I've said hello to every customer today." Putting down the tablet, Tori surveyed the store to ensure no patrons lingered within earshot. She needn't have worried. Now that their faithful troupe of rental devotees had subsided, a few folks browsed the movies. Others leafed through records and listened to music on headphones. At the rear of the store, Val Wainwright, tonight's third staff member, spoke to Ryan's old football coach about a vintage hi-fi Tori had found at an estate sale.

"Oh, come on, Queen of De Nile," Mer said gently, touching Tori's arm. "We shared an apartment for years. I know you. Chatting with regulars doesn't qualify. We didn't talk much Monday. Val said you seemed down Tuesday and yesterday too. Tell me this isn't about Brett Evans showing up."

"Of course not," Tori fudged.

A customer approached, sparing her from one of Meridy's famous inquisitions. After Meridy's two days off, the younger woman didn't know about Brett's second visit and Tori hadn't decided whether to tell her. Between the electrical updating started on the house this morning and the month-end for her business, her mind and body moved like mud. Discussing Brett would only frustrate her.

Meridy tipped her head toward the man carrying a jazz LP. "I'll take this guy." Her long blond hair flipped over her shoulder as she blasted a high-wattage smile his way.

Tori eased out a breath. *Yi-yi*, Meridy was tenacious. *Thank you, Mr. Jazz Fan, for the save.*

The store door tinkled, and a slender woman sailed inside. "Hello, darlings!" Mrs. Kirk's gray curls flowed over her bohemian blouse as she perched massive sunglasses atop her head.

Tori reached beneath the counter for the new release she'd automatically reserved for the seventy-five-year-old widow. She covered the title with her hand. "Good evening, Mrs. Kirk. How are you?"

"Better than I was yesterday, but not as good as I'll be tomorrow." Mrs. Kirk winked. "My movie-of-the-week club chose the first *Thor* film for tonight's screening, and I can't wait. The scenery is spectacular."

"The special effects, you mean?"

"Not quite, dear." Mrs. Kirk chuckled.

"Ah, the actor." Chris Hemsworth. Mrs. Kirk and her On the Prowl movie club were huge fans.

"I spoke to Val earlier." Mrs. Kirk opened her gargantuan tote. "She put aside a copy. It's all Thor, every week, until we've rewatched the franchise." Her shoulders wriggled.

"Here's the movie," Meridy said, slipping Tori the case. Meridy handed her jazz customer a receipt, and he left.

"Thanks, Mer." Tori looked at Mrs. Kirk. "Remember, it's two-for-one night,"—an old marketing perk their clientele treasured —"which means you can also get *this* one." She placed the latest installment of an erotic trilogy on the counter.

Mrs. Kirk squealed. "Delightful! Tori, you never fail to keep me happy. I hope the store is doing well? It's so lovely to drop in and browse and talk to people who know their stuff. I might be an old fuddy-duddy, but streaming isn't for me. I don't care what my grandson says. He's not a Portland peep. He doesn't know how we roll."

Tori smiled. "You're not a fuddy-duddy. And the store is doing fantastic. Thank you for asking."

Finally, with the addition of the hard-to-find vinyl records and also the vintage and replica hi-fis for sale, the Retro Vibe was performing better than variations of the business had in years. Before too long, Tori would need to hire more staff. Specifically, an audio expert. She wanted every customer to feel like the Retro Vibe was their go-to place for music and movies.

"I'm glad to hear it." Mrs. Kirk punched keys on the credit card device. "We geriatric cougars need our abs-and-pecs fixes too."

Tori laughed. "The new release is due back Saturday by six, but *Thor* is yours for the week. Enjoy the 'scenery,' Mrs. Kirk." The door tinkled behind the pleasant woman.

Meridy wagged a finger beneath Tori's nose. "There's the cheerful girl I know and love."

"Sorry. It's that time of month. Makes me grumpy."

"Uh-huh." Meridy's gaze drifted to Val, heading to the counter. An expressive brunette who carried her generous curves with style, Val worked Tuesday through Thursday with the odd Friday or Saturday thrown in. Tori had known both women since high school, although Val was a year older and Meridy a year younger.

"How did it go with Mr. Weldon?" Tori asked Val.

"Pretty good. He wants to bring in his wife to have a look at the piece. He's browsing records now." Val leaned on the counter, silver bangles clinking. "Two customers are looking at movies, and the Thor clone wants to rent a gaming system for the rest of June. Can you believe it? Who does that?"

"Thor clone?" Tori exchanged an amused glance with Meridy. "Is Mrs. Kirk rubbing off on you, Val?"

"No, I swear, this guy looks like a combo of Chris Hemsworth and a young Brad Pitt. Tall, great shoulders, blond hair. Think Pitt in Clooney's *Ocean's Eleven* trilogy but not as scruffy. Hemsworth with Pitt dimples and short hair—that's our guy."

"Yum." Meridy smacked her lips. "When did he come in?"

"You were grabbing lattes. Tori was in her office."

"Damn bookkeeping," Tori mumbled.

"He's way in back," Val added. "Weekly games. There. He's walking toward Stan Weldon with an armload of them. I wonder if they know each other?"

Tori and Meridy rose on their toes. Tori caught a glimpse of a white dress shirt, gray trousers, and short-trimmed blond hair. The gaming customer's head turned as he reached Mr. Weldon.

Prickling sensations suffused her body. She clomped back onto her feet. "He doesn't look like a young Brad Pitt. He *is* the pits," she muttered.

Val's eyebrows bunched. "Huh?"

No offense to Val's powers of observation, but Brett was more rugged-looking than the actor at any age. Also taller. Bigger hands. Subtler dimples. A sexier smile. A kiss that could melt off Tori's bra. And *had.*

"That's Brett Evans," she whispered. "What's he doing here?" A question she never seemed to stop asking herself lately.

"The cherry picker," Meridy whispered to Val, blue eyes sparkling.

Val's jaw dropped. "*That* Brett? I missed a lot popping out three kids in a row. Holy cow, he's hot." Val fanned a hand over her face.

"Renting a gaming system for a month will cost him a fortune." Tori shoved her tablet onto a ledge beneath the counter. "His hotel might offer machines in his room. Why come here?" Days had passed with no contact. What did he want? He was driving her insane!

"He mentioned staying at a hotel," Val said. "How did you know?"

The store door tinkled, and a familiar mother with two girls entered, digging Tori another escape tunnel. The woman asked for help finding an animated classic, and Meridy accompanied the chattering family to the Kids' Corner.

Val slipped behind the counter. "Wade hasn't touched me in weeks. Gimme something juicy, Tori, please."

Tori drew in a breath. This was no big deal. In fact, she would prove how *little* a deal it was by confiding in Val while Brett remained occupied with Stan Weldon.

She outlined the events of Sunday and Monday. Val's brown gaze softened.

"Sweetie, the way he suddenly appeared at your house brought back the hurt. Tori, I'm not sure how to tell you, but you're stuck in the past."

Tori tensed. "I'm not stuck on anything." Her voice rang hollow. "He is."

"Yes, you are. I lied about Wade, by the way. We did it last night."

Tori swatted her arm. *"You."*

Val's mouth curved.

Meridy reappeared with the mother and two girls. After the family left, Val crooked a finger. Tori and Meridy lowered their heads.

"Think about it, Tori," Val half-whispered. "You salivated over this man for years but only got one night with his hot bod. And Kendall What's-Her-Name, the lawyer he lived with before Ryan's wedding? What happened there?"

"Kendall Brandt," Tori whispered. She glanced Brett's direction. He and Mr. Weldon appeared engaged in lively conversation. Pulse racing, she divulged, "The way B was with Kendall is how he handles all his relationships, last I knew."

During Ryan's engagement, Giselle and her bridesmaids had dished about each groomsman at one time or another. In Tori's state of Brett-adoration, she'd soaked up every detail. "With B, it was a friends-with-benefits arrangement or nothing." And if, in

Brett's estimation, he made 'a mistake,' like he claimed he had with Tori, then apparently it was *sayonara* and fast-forward a few years to the insulting 'pals' stage. "They—Brett and Kendall— were both focused on their careers. Living together was"—she shrugged—"I don't know...handy. Basically, they would come home from work, say howdy-do, and get horizontal if the mood struck. No long talks about each other's lives, no walks in the rain, or romantic dinners."

Meridy flipped a hand. "That's better than being a player."

Then why did Tori feel played?

A soundtrack drifted from the shop speakers, serving as valuable cover.

She continued in quiet tones, "About four months before Ryan's wedding, B invited K as his plus-one. K said yes, but then the company B now works for in Sacramento headhunted him, and next thing you know, he was making plans to move to California. So K vamoosed, sticking him with their lease."

"I've heard this part before, and I don't get it," Meridy said, head and voice low. "If K knew B was heading to Cali, and they were only friends-with-bennies sharing rent and utilities, why not ride things out? Why dump him months ahead?"

Val gave a wry smile. "Wedding preparations bring out weird behavior in couples. Maybe K didn't want him to catch a proposal-bug. Like a virus."

"In a way." Tori held a hand against the side of her face to block Brett's view of her mouth, in case he'd developed long-distance lip-reading skills. "B took being Ryan's best man seriously. He asked K's advice about wedding stuff. Did she like his tux? What gift should he buy? Would she attend the rehearsal dinner? To hear Giselle talk, K felt like she and B were becoming too comfortable and settled or something. K wasn't about to move to California, even if he asked. She did what she thought best, and he wasn't heartbroken." Tori glanced to the rear of the store. *Still safe.* Guilt sluiced through her. She shouldn't gossip about Brett's personal life. Except it was her life too, and these women were her friends.

Meridy raised a finger. "Then *you* began making moves on the hot guy suddenly lacking a plus-one."

"Why, Tori." Val poked her shoulder. "You vixen."

"I didn't consciously trick him into taking my V," Tori whispered. "He was single, and I was smitten. It felt like fate." Which sounded dumb, in retrospect.

"How do you feel about everything now?" Val asked.

"Edgy. You know me, I don't hold grudges. I *thought* I didn't. I thought that night with Brett was buried and done."

Meridy checked over her shoulder. "Tori, don't pin this on yourself. You have the biggest heart I know."

The organ in question throbbed. "Right now it feels dark and shriveled." Ornery Tori was taking over her life.

Meridy gazed at her. "Have you considered your man troubles might be related to unresolved feelings for Brett?'

Tori sneered. "Man troubles?"

"Unless there's something you haven't told me, you haven't been with a guy since Cory."

"Don't remind me." Cory Price, the super-nice, super-compatible grocery store manager she had dated a year—her personal record on the romantic front. Everyone had said it was cute their names rhymed. That Cory and Tori were cute together. Her mom had mentioned the possibility of cute grandkids, a cute carload of them with those cute cartoon stickers on the rear windshield, living in a cute house with cute shutters and a cute cottage-shaped mailbox.

Cute, cute, cute!

Tori and Cory nearly fell for all the feels their friends and family had expressed.

But once they'd discussed getting engaged, they'd realized cute rhyming names and lukewarm loving wasn't enough. Tori hadn't dated in the seven months since their amicable split.

Considering everything on her plate—renovating the house, the development of the store, adopting Rex, her brother's divorce—she'd needed a break from searching for Mr. Right. At this point, she couldn't handle another disappointment.

Meridy half-whispered, "Maybe you're subconsciously attracting the wrong type of guy because you're not finished with this one—Brett."

Val whacked the counter. "Eureka!"

"Shh," Tori whispered. "He'll hear us."

Her heart banged. She darted her gaze across the store. Brett, holding the gaming discs, finished talking to Mr. Weldon and stepped toward the replica turntables, several feet closer. Juggling the discs, he lifted the wood lid of a table-top model and examined the innards.

"He can't hear us." Meridy squeezed Tori's hand. "I followed a link about something like this the other day. Maybe you need to work Brett out of your system before you can move on. Your one night together whet your appetite. Now you need the whole buffet. He's in town for a month, right? It's the perfect opportunity."

Tori rolled her eyes. "What would you suggest I do, Meridy? Jump his bones?"

Val snapped her fingers. "Yes! Seduce him. For revenge!"

"That's cruel," Tori whispered. And vaguely soap-opera-ish.

"Not revenge," Meridy replied. "*Closure*. You want a hot, healthy relationship with a guy who deserves you. You might never find that if you don't resolve your feelings for Brett."

Tori shook her head. "You two are crazy."

Meridy's gaze flitted away. "Bachelor alert." She gripped Tori's arm. "B and another guy are coming. Pretend we're exchanging recipes." She whipped out her phone. "I'll find one."

Tori's pulse gathered speed. Recipes? *Good luck*. Images of a stark-naked Brett flooded her mind. A stab of ancient hurt followed.

Damn it, she hated harboring these festering feelings of resentment. She liked being cheerful, hard-working Tori. Capable of forgiveness. Optimistic about the future. Knowing deep inside that her timing might be off but eventually she would nail love. That there was hope.

If only Brett weren't so clueless, barging in on her carefully ordered life. So sincere and good-looking and oblivious. So...*Brett.*

Val patted her arm. "I'll intercept him. Meridy, you catch the first customer."

Tori swallowed. "Thanks, guys." She faced the computer.

❦

Brett neared the counter, balancing a heap of gaming discs. He didn't recognize half the titles and hell if his busy schedule allowed time to play video games. Renting the system for the remainder of June would gobble a huge chunk of change. Expensing the cost to DataPrimer was out of the question. This was personal, part of his quest toward convincing Tori he was a good guy.

"So suck it up, Buttercup," he mumbled beneath his breath.

Tori had stopped talking to her employees and turned away. Looked like her cold shoulder hadn't warmed. Three days had passed. She had to forgive him sometime. But what if she never did?

He pushed the possibility to the cluttered recesses of his over-taxed mind. He needed her in his life. Too bad it had taken four years and two bottles of water drenching his clothes to wake him up.

The brunette clerk walked over. "I'll help you, sir."

"Thanks." Brett handed the woman the games, and stepped behind the U-shaped counter. A crew of college-aged kids spilled inside the store, jabbering about cool vinyl records. The blond clerk corralled them toward the LPs, and a customer from moments ago left.

With an eye on Tori's back, Brett opened his wallet. "How's it going?" He checked the brunette's nametag. "Val. Beautiful day."

Tori's spine stiffened. Her loose hair shielded her face as she muttered something to Val.

Val nodded. Her gaze returned to Brett. "It sure is. A little hot for this time of year. We could use some rain."

A smile tugged Brett's mouth. Portlanders possessed a penchant for precipitation. He didn't mind the wet stuff, but years out of state had acclimated him to the shining yellow orb in the sky.

"I'll need your driver's license and a credit card for renting the gaming system, please," Val said.

"It's a California license."

"That's okay. Tori said she knows you. We'll also require the name, address, and phone number of your hotel."

"Can do. I'm changing places in a couple of days. Will you need the new info?"

"Um?" Val's gaze skipped to her boss.

Tori's fingers drummed the counter.

"I'll call the store once I've moved hotels." Then Tori would have the details at her dancing fingertips, in addition to his cell number and email address. A happy outcome, in the event she'd shredded his business card. He placed his ID on the counter. "I'd like to rent the newest model of the gaming system." The most expensive brand in the store.

"Great." Val shot another glance to Tori. "Do you want to fetch the machine, or shall I?"

Tori whirled around. "That system will cost a mint to rent for a month, Brett, even with an extended-use discount. Why not buy one?"

He glanced at nearby aisles. "I don't see any for sale."

"Not *here*." She crossed her arms beneath her breasts. They plumped in her V-necked top, displaying cleavage. "Somewhere else. A department store or warehouse place."

"I don't need a discount, and I don't care about cost. I just want to give you the business."

Val's gaze ping-ponged between them. "Should I get the machine?"

The blond clerk swept past. "I'm heading that way." She waved a record. "I'm checking for extra copies of this album. I'll bring out the system."

"Thanks, Meridy," Val said. "Need help with the college kids?"

"Nope. Everything's under control." The blonde disappeared into a stock room.

Tori snatched Brett's ID and methodically inputted his data into the store software. A faint blush blossomed on her face. Brett's gaze lowered to her vibrant blue T-shirt. The silver threads of the Retro Vibe logo perched in the vicinity of her curvaceous heart.

"I like the new colors of the place. The silver lettering pops." A DataPrimer colleague talked decorating non-stop. He'd learned some lingo during long hours poring over computer code.

Tori's nipples flicked into high beam. Frenzied fingers flew over the keyboard.

Val planted a hand on her hip. "You're staring at her boobs, pal. Not cool."

Brett whipped up his gaze. "Tori and I are friends. I'm not interested in her breas—uh, boobs." His neck heated.

Val's eyebrows arched. "Honey, if you're breathing and straight, you're interested." She murmured to Tori, "Forget closure. He deserves the other."

"Stop it, Val." Tori's gaze remained glued to the computer screen.

"Deserves what?" Brett asked.

"To be hit over the head for that comment," Val said.

Brett frowned. Was Val implying he insulted Tori by stating

disinterest in her secondary sex characteristics? This Val woman didn't know him, although she clearly knew *about* him. Had Tori discussed his arrival with her employees? Were the women friends?

"Naturally, I'm interested in her breasts," he backpedaled, checking to ensure no customers stood within hearing distance. "In an aesthetic sense. That is to say, I think they—that all female parts—uh, that Tori's, in particular, are nice." A generic enough description.

Val laughed and moved to the second machine to ring in a customer. "Okay, Prince Charming. You've won me over."

It wasn't Val he needed to win over.

Tori keyed in his hotel details, gazing at him from beneath lowered lashes. Was she reevaluating his slug status?

She slid his ID across the counter. Her mouth tipped upward ever so slightly. "I've arranged a weekly price for the gaming system. Sound fair?"

Not wanting to lose the marginally warmer atmosphere, Brett caved on the pricing issue. "Say, what happened to the loft?" During his and Ryan's childhood and adolescence, a staircase led to a space at the upper rear of the store, which initially housed more movies and games. Later, video arcades and pool tables populated the loft. Now, a ceiling sealed off the upstairs. "Ry and I had a blast stealing old Mr. Folk's snooker balls and selling them back to him to buy gumballs."

Tori smiled. Brett held a breath. Was he making progress?

"Mr. Folk wasn't old. He just went bald young."

Brett shuddered. "Don't mention hair loss. My father is a mosquito airport." He didn't care to resemble Hank Evans in *any* manner.

Tori's lips twitched. "Isn't baldness usually carried in the mother's genes? I've seen pictures of your uncles. You're not in danger." Her fingertips fluttered. "Some bald guys are really sexy. If you start losing hair, just don't let the crown thing grow around your ears. That's what ages men. Shave everything off. Then there's no issue."

"I'll keep that in mind." Bald guys were sexy?

Rose streaked her cheeks. "Anyway, Dad put in ceiling joists and partitioned off the second floor for offices he and Ry are constructing this fall."

"That's an excellent idea. How many spaces?"

"Three. They'll share a stairwell and a separate entrance at the back of the building. We plan on leasing them."

Brett stuffed his ID into his wallet. "How long does your mom plan to keep working?"

Tori's shoulders lifted. "Whatever she wants. I'm flexible."

Yes, he remembered her dexterity from that long-ago night.

"Eventually, I'll assume full-time management of the store. Mom and Dad will continue to receive dividends. All four of us have a vested interest in the building."

Brett nodded. Tori knew what she wanted, and she went for it. Full blast, all the way.

"A store *and* a house. That's a lot for twenty-six."

"The Bank of Mom and Dad are a big help. They're mortgage-free. I made a down payment, and each month I transfer funds to their account. It saves oodles in interest."

"Don't feel you need to justify how your family operates. It's admirable." Brett tapped his wallet on the counter. Where was the blond clerk with his gaming system? "I recognized one of your employees. Not Val. The other girl." From where, he hadn't a clue.

"Meridy Ashworth." Tori rearranged a display of Retro Vibe gift cards. "Her older sister Samara and I were tight in high school. Sam moved to Seattle for college and stayed. Mer and I began hanging around. We're now closer than Sam and I ever were."

Now they were talking—as in *really* talking. This might be his last chance to set things right. He needed to make the most of it.

49

"I ran into Samara a time or two while attending U-Dub," he recalled with a smile. "And I seem to remember spotting you and Meridy at a club in the Pearl district when I was home visiting Mom. Meridy had a fake ID, and you were barely twenty-one."

Tori avoided his gaze. "You introduced us to your girlfriend."

Not his *girlfriend*. His friend-with-benefits. It was an important distinction. He didn't do serious relationships. Not the sort Tori deserved, requiring emotional commitment. He gave the benefits thing a whirl every year or so, blowing off steam with a like-minded woman for a few months until one of them felt the need to bury their heads in work again.

"You wore a bluey-green dress. It tied in a bow"—he tapped the back of his neck—"beneath your hair."

"It's called turquoise, Evans. Halter-style."

"Well, the color popped." As had his fantasies for several weeks afterward. His FWB relationship fizzled around the same time.

A customer stepped to the counter. Brett's stack of games still sat beside the register. He moved out of line until Meridy returned.

"Sorry," she said, placing the gaming case next to Tori's elbow. "I got hung up."

"No problem." Tori pushed the system aside.

Carrying several records, Meridy headed for the college kids.

Brett reached the front. Tori pushed the gaming system further away. Then she stared at the case, grasped it, and deposited it on the floor inside the counter.

"I'll be needing that," he said.

"Not anymore." She fiddled with an earring. "I've decided you can stay at the house. Ry stored his gaming gear and wide-screen in the rec room. You can use them."

Brett's heart thundered with the force of a bowling ball catapulting toward a strike. "Tori, don't feel guilty about this. At all.

We can learn to be friends again without living under the same roof."

She shook her head. "Ry said you could stay, so you will. Mom and Dad had an open-door policy where you were concerned. But don't get too excited. I'm not microwaving frozen pizza or stocking up on bacon and cereal. It's just a place to stay." She ran two fingers through her hair. "And…you can lend a hand with the renovations now and then, like you said Monday."

The tension in his shoulders eased. "What changed your mind?" Ten minutes ago, she'd looked like she'd wanted to lop off his head.

"You keep surprising me, and I needed time to think."

Brett's smile stretched across his face. The three-day break had worked. Now he had the green light to spend the rest of the month getting to know her again. A bittersweet sensation pinged in his chest. *This* was the Tori he'd missed. Generous. Caring. Flexible.

She cleared her throat. "You can sleep in my old room. I'm in the master now."

"I'll take the attic." Ry's old room. "You'll have more privacy." Only the main-floor bathroom separated her childhood room from the master. "A second shower is in the basement, as I remember."

"It needs retiling, and my living room furniture is stored in the attic. Use my old room. We'll share the bathroom."

"I don't want to be a pain in the ass. I'll sleep on the rec room couch."

"Too late on the PITA, Evans. My old room has the second door. If you use the kitchen one most of the time and also the back porch for coming and going, I'll have all the privacy I need."

"Okay." They were actually having a civil conversation. Amazing. "I am paying for the game rentals. And I insist on paying the same room and board I meant for your parents."

She glanced toward the rear of the store. "Look at that. The teens are choosing a turntable. Meridy needs help. I gotta go." Hurrying past him, she touched his arm. His skin burned as her fingertips grazed his shirtsleeve. "You can move in Saturday. You were changing hotels then anyway, right? That allows me a day to prep my old room. We'll settle details later." Butt bouncing, she scampered away.

Brett peeled his gaze off her perky rear. His neck hairs bristled. He turned.

Val studied him from the counter. Not a single customer stood in line.

His gaze widened. "What?"

"Cute tush, huh?" the woman asked in a quiet yet moderately sinister, devil-on-his-shoulder voice.

"Whose?" Brett's irises sizzled like frying eggs, but he refused to break eye contact.

Her head jerked Tori's direction. "I think you know."

"I wasn't staring." Just taking note.

"Whatever you say." Val's gaze zeroed in on his face, her expression jarringly reminiscent of a mob boss ordering a hit. "She's doing you a favor, allowing you to stay at her house. Don't blow this, Hot Stuff. Don't break her heart."

"You don't need to tell me that. I'm here to patch things up."

"Words, pal." Val flicked two fingers between her eyes and his. "I've got spies everywhere."

And antennae hidden beneath her hair, he supposed—his mother's favorite expression for encouraging good behavior.

"Noted. Now can I pay for my games?"

Val smiled. "Of course, sir. Thank you." She whisked the bills from his hand.

Collecting the discs, Brett strolled out the door. Val was as subtle as a mama bear, but her message merited serious consideration. Everything he wanted for his month in Portland lay within reach. A relaxing home instead of another anonymous hotel room. Meals cooked on the alien appliance most people referred to as a stove. A cheerful face greeting him at the end of a long day.

A dog to walk. A to-do list, complete with colorful doodles.

And Tori, his pal since childhood.

He wouldn't cross that boundary again.

4

"COME ON, TEABISCUIT, put a little muscle into it," Tori mumbled into the industrial-grade dust mask covering her nose and mouth. How did Darth Vader manage his breathing device, fictional-character-latitude aside? She couldn't drag enough air into her lungs. Add her dad's heavy safety goggles and earmuffs to the mix, and she was lucky she could hold up her head.

Astride a wobbly dinette chair, she slid the electric mouse sander along the mahogany crown molding. The long piece of shaped wood balanced on her leg, one end resting on a padded cloth covering the concrete workshop floor. A real bright idea, buying the palm sander. She'd pictured the pointed tip gracefully sweeping inward curves. What a joke. Her right shoulder ached, a sticky-tape sensation layered both eyes, and perspiration saturated her sweats and T-shirt.

Blinking in rapid succession, she repositioned the molding, slapped a new piece of sandpaper onto the mouse, and tried again. The oily scent of melting varnish floated around the cordoned-off sanding area as orangey-brown dust particles powdered her sneakers. She soldiered on, air wheezing in and out of her chest.

Lordy-Lou, it felt like she'd been wrong about everything today and last night at the store. Wrong about the sander purchase. Wrong about imagining she might work through her issues with Brett by allowing him to stay at her house and then emerge from the experience unscathed. Upbeat Tori once more focused on the future, ready to embrace the perfect guy when he happened along. *If* he happened along.

She must have been crazy.

She needed to obliterate Ornery Tori, but, honest to God, what had possessed her to honor Ry's arrangement as a solution? How about downing a bottle of chill pills instead?

A long three and a half weeks remained in Brett's consulting contract with Sugartree Electric. Twenty-six days, beginning tomorrow. She'd tallied the total in her planner.

Twenty-six nights.

Twenty-six days and nights of sharing the same bathroom and kitchen. Of seeing his toothbrush beside hers in the cup and catching whiffs of his aftershave in a bottle on the up-john shelf. Of sleeping one bedroom and a short hall's distance from the handsome cherry picker who wanted nothing more than to be her platonic pal.

She applied more pressure to the sander. Who was he trying to kid? A woman sensed vibrations of attraction emanating from interested guys, and Brett's weren't malfunctioning. Last night at the store, she'd caught the fascinated glint in his eyes when he'd thought she wasn't looking. Really, did he gawk at *male* pecs at the gym? It wasn't like he could flip a switch and become asexual only around her.

She grabbed another chunk of mouse paper. Her shoulder cramped and her head pounded, but, at last, she ground off most of the thick varnish and stain. Tackling the inward curves required old-fashioned hand-sanding. A job for another day. And just think, after sanding four whole slats tonight, a measly three dozen moldings, baseboards, and door and window trims remained.

Tori carted the long length of molding to her teensy Stage Two pile and extricated her matted ponytail from the dust mask. A coughing fit ensued.

After stripping to her clammy bra and panties, she parted the polythene curtains surrounding the sanding station and trudged barefoot up to the kitchen. The stove clock declared twenty past midnight. Rex slept in his cozy house on the back porch, safe from inhaling specks of varnish and irritating his sensitive beagle snout.

In the bathroom, she glimpsed her reflection above the sink. Indentations from the workshop mask tracked her cheeks. Sanding dust coated her hair.

"Charming." She cocked her eyebrows at the goofus in the mirror. "Like spice cake mix exploded on your head."

If Brett were here now, he wouldn't stay long. He'd run screaming down the street. Her mouth quirked. There was an idea—terrify the guy into leaving early.

Except what would that accomplish? She would still be Ornery Tori, nowhere near prepared for meeting CHAD, her acronym for her future husband. Caring, Honest, Attractive Dad-material.

Or, as Val teased, Cute and Horny, with abundant Abs, Dammit.

Sighing, Tori unfastened her ponytail and peeled her bra and panties to the floor. Were Meridy and Val right? Did she have unfinished business with her brother's best friend? Was her truncated night of passion with Brett Hennessy Evans responsible for why she and Cory had ultimately resembled a text-it-in relationship? Why every boyfriend before and since her visit to Brett's hotel room somehow fell short of the mark?

Meridy might have uncovered a reality Tori hadn't possessed

the temerity to confront on her own. One night with Brett *had* whet her appetite, but how could she ever manage to gorge on the yummy Evans buffet?

Tears stung her eyes as her thoughts tumbled over and over. How could she open her heart to loving CHAD, to building a future with oh-so-worth-the-wait CHAD, if *any* part of her yearned for Brett?

What the panic attack was she going to do?

Inhaling raggedly, she stepped into the tub and lifted her face to the hot shower spray. Cleansing water sluiced over her scalp and body. For several minutes, she splashed relaxing warmth over her face and sore neck, massaged her tender right shoulder, and stretched her spine. She raked fingers through her sodden hair until gummy residue no longer caked her follicles. Two shampoos, a round of conditioner, then soap, hands skimming her heated skin. Her breasts and tummy. Between her legs.

Her breathing quickened, and an image blossomed in her mind. She envisioned Brett's hands gliding over the same territory her fingers explored, but not for washing. Oh, no. She visualized them sharing a shower after making love in the big hotel bed. In tonight's heavily revised version of Four Years Ago, his stunned expression upon discovering her virginity didn't exist.

He's moving in tomorrow, a tiny voice broke into her sensual mist. *I can't.*

Tori's eyes flickered open. Screw *can't*. This was *her* fantasy, and she intended to carpe-diem all over the place.

She closed her eyes again as the hot water streamed. Shower Brett joined her beneath the spray. She would gratify him *and* herself.

For CHAD...

Brett lathered her body head to toe. Tori's sensitized skin trembled as he slid the tiny bar of perfumed hotel soap back onto the shelf in the double-wide stall with the rainforest shower head. Desire glimmered in his blue,

blue eyes, the lashes thick, masculine, and gorgeous, his smile wickedly tempting.

Tori smiled in return, eager to convey her love and need. She'd saved herself for a moment like this.

For this man.

For Brett.

His erection twitched.

She wrapped her hand around the stiff length. He moaned and kissed her, hands cupping her face before sliding over her breasts and hips…

A keening cry escaped her lips. Exquisite tingling sensations powered to her center, zooming along her limbs, and blasting out her fingertips and toes. Her pulse zip-lined into outer space.

"CHAD," she whispered on a raggedy gasp. "You better appreciate my sacrifice."

She emerged from the shower on rubbery legs and dried off. Robe nestling her shoulders, she brushed her teeth until the minty paste foamed at the corners of her mouth.

Brett had reduced her to this frothing insanity.

"Meridy and Val are right," she muttered around her toothpaste-slathered tongue. "I'm not finished with him." She spit out foam and attacked her gums, stomach roiling along with the vigorous swipes.

Brett's business card remained on her kitchen counter, his cell number announcing itself in exasperating glory. One quick text message would retract Ry's invitation to stay at the house, but why bother? If the past few days were anything to go by, Brett would quadruple his efforts to become her pal. All his earnest sincerity was simply too much too late.

Rinsing her mouth and plunking the toothbrush in its receptacle cup, she retreated to the master bedroom and selected a pretty spiral-bound notebook from the small desk she and Mick had moved in from her old room. Purple hand-lettering adorned a space on the patterned cover:

RENOVATIONS

The contents amounted to three pages of sketches and notes. Tori had tested the notebook for her summer remodeling endeavors before splurging on a beautiful leather zippered planner with pockets for receipts as well as blank, lined, and dotted pages to diagram, chart her progress, and brainstorm future renovations.

Sitting on the bed, damp hair drying in chunks against her robe, she uncapped a thin purple marker and slashed a line through RENOVATIONS. She added a couple of swirls for decorative flourish.

Below the old title, she drew in funky lettering, *Dealing With Brett. DWB.*

She gazed at the script, dissatisfaction whirling in her veins. DWB reminded her of FWB, her acronym for Brett's annoying friends with benefits philosophy.

She scratched out the new title—adding a flourish—and tried Closure With Brett. *CWB.*

Her nose scrunched. *Bah.*

Preparing for CHAD, she wrote. *PFCHAD.*

Nope.

Getting *Through* Brett *to* CHAD. *GTBTCHAD.*

Accurate, but too many consonants.

She needed a real word. Something with action. Or at least pizzazz.

She attempted, *Getting* Over *Brett. GOB.*

A snicker slipped past her lips. The heading wasn't precisely true, but the letters produced a satisfying acronym.

She flipped to an empty page and chose a fuchsia pen from her collection. Ink poised to paper, she recorded the date and wrote:

He wants to be pals? To treat me like one of the guys? If he were female, the equivalent of a sorority sister.

As if our genders plain old don't matter?

Where does that leave me?

She tapped the pen against her nose. Inspiration struck. Fuchsia handwriting looped across the page.

I'll treat him like one of the girls.

Brett wandered down the short hall to the combination living/dining room, the mug of mid-morning coffee Tori had offered upon his arrival twenty minutes ago warming his hand. Rex flanked his right, canine lips turned up in what Brett swore was a smile. The young beagle had shadowed Brett while he'd stowed his socks and jeans in Tori's childhood dresser and hung his shirts and pants in the same small closet which had held her clothes for years.

Setting his shaving cream next to her hairbrush on the bathroom shelf had struck him as a trifle intimate. Same with noticing her personal items. Cotton balls and nail polish remover. Multi-colored bath capsules. A couple of burned candles. A tiny basket of elastics.

Was he doing the right thing, forging into an unknown future with Tori in an effort to recapture an elusive *je ne sais quoi* from their youths?

The feminine touches to the bathroom announced loud and clear that her tastes as an adult ran more girly than he remembered. As a kid, she had been more of a tomboy. As a teen, what his mother had called a late bloomer. For Brett, treating her like a stand-in little sister had felt like second nature...until she began growing up.

He shook off his disquieting thoughts. He needed to focus on the goal at hand. Against all odds, Tori had changed her mind about moving forward with their friendship, inviting him to share her comfortable, if half-dismantled, home. He intended to repay her generosity.

"Tori?" He swept his gaze to the swinging door open to the kitchen. A squat stool secured the base. The homey scent of the banana-nut muffins Tori had mentioned baking drifted in on the unseasonably warm air. "I'm unpacked," he said, glancing left. "Should I walk R—?"

Sweet mercy. His feet glued to the floor, heart thudding. He blinked to clear his vision. Tori knelt beneath the picture window, bowing like a religious supplicant, her head lowered and her forearms resting on the carpet. Her floral T-shirt rode up the small of her back, exposing an inch of decidedly non-supplicant skin, and her rear bobbed in cut-off sweats the color of ripe peaches while she inspected…whatever she inspected.

Twenty minutes ago, she had worn jeans.

The cut-offs displayed a hint of tan on her lean, strong legs. Brett conjured up a memory of Tori at fourteen speeding the bases during springtime neighborhood softball games.

At twenty-one, in the Pearl District nightclub, her silky dress had swirled at her thighs.

At twenty-two, those supple legs had wrapped around his waist, her eager voice driving him wild despite her secrecy about her virginity.

A muscle ticked beneath one eye. And then he'd hurt her.

Val's mobster warning at the store two days ago mushroomed in his mind: *Don't blow this, Hot Stuff. Don't break her heart.*

Tori's friend was haunting him.

Maybe that was a good thing. While he didn't strictly require a reminder, it couldn't hurt to keep Val's reprimand front and center. Tori wasn't a woman to enjoy for a few weeks of no-strings sex. With her caring heart and deep ties to family and community, she was born to be a wife and mother. A forever lover.

And he wasn't a forever type of guy.

Beside him, Rex wagged his tail before scampering across the room and nosing Tori's leg. She glanced over her shoulder, gaze meeting Brett's.

"Oh. Hi." Her hand flapped in a wilted wave, as if Brett were a mosquito or other insect to dismiss. "Is Rex bothering you?"

"Nah, he's cute." The goofball dog had personality. Sipping his coffee, Brett strolled closer. "What are you doing?"

Rising to her knees, she dusted off her hands. "Deciding how to lift the carpet tacks. Dad preferred the warmth of carpet beneath his feet for watching TV, but original oak is under this beige wall-to-wall."

The two bedrooms and the hall floors featured hardwood. "The carpet seems in decent shape."

"Yes, but Dad doesn't live here anymore. I want to put my own stamp on the place." Rex dug his snout into her hip and whined. Laughing softly, she fondled the dog's ears. "The floor needs refinishing. Scratches and worn wood are way easier to sand out than gouges." She grabbed a rubber handball and tossed it across the carpet. The blue orb sailed past Brett's sock-covered feet. "Don't catch the ball. Rex chases it."

The beagle whipped across the room. Brett grinned. "Atta boy. No wimpy doggy toys for him."

"Rex destroys most dog toys in two days or less. Beagles have very strong teeth. He has some stuffies, but handballs are the best exercise inside the house I've discovered."

"I couldn't interest him in a game of stick in the park the other day."

"Outdoor scents distract him. He wants to sniff, not fetch. Inside, it's the handball or playing tug of war with his knotted rope or a stuffy." Tori plucked the scooped neckline of her T-shirt from her chest, distracting Brett. "I wish this heat would cut us some slack. I hate dragging out summer clothes before July, but it's seriously hot."

"You bet she is," the mini-Val perched on Brett's shoulder muttered. *"Eyes north, chump."*

Struggling not to twitch, he set his coffee mug on the windowsill. "Let's look at those carpet tacks."

Rex dashed back with the handball. "Drop," Tori ordered, and the ball plopped into her palm. She lobbed the toy across the room again, and Rex whizzed off, breath huffing.

Gingerly, Tori lifted a section of carpet. Sharp black tacks jutted from a thin strip of wood nailed into the oak floor. She explained, "The carpet releases easily. Rolling it up won't be a problem. If I'm careful prying out the nails"—she touched the strip resting on hardwood—"the refinished baseboards will cover the resulting holes. I'll need to tap a flathead screwdriver or something similar under the tack strips to lift them." Her forehead crinkled. "If I damage the floor, the baseboards won't cover the scars and I'll need to putty in spots. Not my first choice."

"Why not leave the carpet tacks where they are and hammer the baseboards to cover the strips?" Brett suggested as Rex ran back and delivered the ball at his feet with an excited yap. Brett tossed the toy toward a skeleton wall. The beagle pounced, snatching the rolling toy and disappearing into the kitchen.

"I don't want to risk splitting the old wood. If I leave the tacks, the edges of the slats might show and the baseboards won't fit snugly to the floor."

"Spoken like the daughter of a hardware man." As a child, she had spent more time with her mom at Jarrett's Video than at her dad's store where Brett and Ryan had worked during high school summers, but Marty Jarrett had supervised the trio of kids through plenty of projects in the basement workshop.

"Dad taught me a lot. I also bought books and stalk how-to videos online. I can rent a sander for the floors, but the wood in these old houses is denser than floors installed in new homes.

Something to do with the age of the trees makes old oak more difficult to sand."

Brett nodded. "On Monday you said these baseboards hail from the thirties. The trees cut for your floors must have been ancient, Tori. Maybe even virgin."

A blush splashed her face.

"Uh, forest." *Smooth, Evans. Remind her what she gave up for you.*

Returning her attention to the floor, she examined the exposed oak. "It's probably best to hire a professional." Her shoulders sagged. "Everyone I called is booked for the summer, and I can't spare the money anyway."

Preparing to stand, she pressed the toes of one sneakered foot to the carpet. Brett extended a hand. She hesitated before grasping his palm.

Small calluses dotted the base of her fingers, a testament to her hard work on the house. His thumb itched to slide over the bumps.

"What the hell?" the mini-Val in his brain barked. *"They're hands, bucko."*

He was well aware. Sue him for having a Y chromosome. These hands had touched his privates.

Tori stood, the floral scent of her soap—or a bath capsule?—carrying to his nostrils. He released her fingers. A wisp of hair wriggled free of her ponytail. She tugged down the ragged hems of her shorts.

Lust speared him.

Mini-Val squawked like a psychotic hen.

Brett firmed his jaw. *Stand down, Val. I've got this.*

"Tori, I wish you'd accept the same room and board I meant to pay your parents. DataPrimer reimburses living expenses. I won't be out of pocket."

Her gaze shifted to her dog trotting in from the kitchen. Rex settled on the fireplace hearth, lodged the handball between his speckled white paws, and chewed.

"I don't want your money, Brett."

"*DataPrimer's* money," he repeated. "You can put the cash toward the renovations."

She shook her head, ponytail swaying. "I'm not using my old room other than for a spot on the bed for Rex to nap every now and again, and you can't eat that much."

"Oh, yeah? Remember Ry and me pigging out on ribs and pizza?"

She punched his shoulder. "Don't worry. You'll work off your food debt."

Brett crossed his arms over his T-shirt. "I see. You want my body."

Her eyes widened. "Excuse me?"

"For free labor. To assist with the renovations." Would that night always stand between them? "We'll start with the carpet tacks and go from there."

Tugging on her shorts again, she nibbled a thumbnail on her other hand. "Can we lift the slats without damaging the floor?"

"Carpet tacks aren't on my resume, but if we put our heads together, we can figure it out." Side-by-side. Friends. Renovation partners.

She drew in a breath, and the swelling of her breasts lured his gaze to her T-shirt. Her Retro Vibe tops weren't as snug.

Kneecapping the dangerous train of thought before mini-Val emerged to do him serious harm, Brett rubbed a hand in circles over his stomach. "Those muffins smell fantastic. Want to grab a bite before getting to work?"

Her mouth curved. "Banana-nut is Meridy's favorite. I bake them for her every Saturday." She fidgeted with her ponytail. "Except this batch is for you. And me. For both of us." Her smile wavered but held.

Brett paused. "Is me staying here weird?"

Her eyes narrowed. "You said you wanted to stay."

"I do. But are you uncomfortable having me around?"

Two fingers plucked the hem of her shorts. "Do I look uncomfortable?"

He restrained a smile. "A little." Like the proverbial ants were marching a picket line inside her too-short pants.

She folded her arms, tucking her hands beneath them. "Well, it has nothing to do with you. Baking the muffins reminds me of Meridy. We lived together six years. I miss her sometimes."

"She works at the store." Didn't they see each other several times a week?

"It's not the same."

"Ask her to move in." After he returned to Sacramento.

Her gaze glinted. "Brett, stop trying to fix what isn't broken. I get lonely on my own now and then, even with Rex around. Having a roommate is a tough habit to break. Mer likes living close to town. The nightclubs, the art galleries, and food carts appeal to her." She shrugged. "I might find someone in the fall, once I'm finished my current stage of renos. He or she would take the bedroom you're staying in now."

He or she? Brett neutralized his inflection. "You're considering a male roommate?"

"I am fully capable of sharing space with a man without becoming romantically entangled."

"That's not what I meant." Except it was.

A far too chipper light brightened her eyes. "You're my test roommate. Guy or girl, it doesn't matter. If I can survive this month with you, I can handle living with another computer nerd. Someone harmless and socially awkward would fit the bill."

Every one of Brett's thirty-three vertebrae stiffened. *Survive this month? Computer nerd? Harmless? Socially awkward?*

She fist-bumped his arm. "So you'll help with the carpet tacks today?"

"Why not?" He clapped his hands. The sooner he broke into a labor-induced sweat, the sooner his fixation on Tori's T-shirt—his *roommate's* T-shirt—would dissipate. "I don't have anything better to do. I'll walk Rex first, if that's okay." He needed to burn off some energy.

She flicked a hand. "I'll walk him. You enjoy the muffins, and we'll start on the carpet tacks in half an hour. Lorelei will be thrilled."

"Lorelei?" How many friends could one woman have?

"Down the street. She wants the carpet for an unfinished room in their basement. Her husband John lost his job, and they can't afford new."

"How much are they paying you?"

Tori laughed. "Nothing. It's a gift. John and another neighbor are lugging out the rug for me, so we're scratching each other's backs. See how that works?"

Brett would happily haul the carpet in his nerdy, harmless, socially awkward manner, but overriding her plans at this stage seemed ill-advised.

"Sounds like you have great neighbors. Must be nice." And a huge stretch from his life in California. He had yet to learn the names of the couple across the hall.

"It is." Tori whistled for her dog. "Rexxy, time for walk."

The beagle scampered to his feet, brown eyes aglitter.

"Where did I leave your leash?" Tori asked Rex as the pair headed for the kitchen. The dog woofed, and she replied, "That's right. By your food bowl."

Her cut-offs rustled in the open doorway. A glimpse of mint-green panties flashed beneath the denim hems.

Brett almost choked on his tongue. Damn it, the woman needed new summer clothes. Any guy she passed on the road would suffer a stroke staring at the wiggle of her sweet behind— and die happy.

Should he follow her and Rex, ensuring no one hassled them?

The noise of the closing porch door suggested a resounding *no*.

If Tori wanted company, she would have invited him along. What she wore was none of his business. Or any other man's.

No one's.

It was no one's business.

Least of all, his.

ori's Planner ~ Thought for the Day
A woman without a plan is just a twit

"WHAT'S THE PLAN, ma'am?" Tori's hottie houseguest asked three days after moving in. He stood to her left at the kitchen counter, spooning chow mein onto her plate. The mouthwatering aroma of Chinese takeout competed with the fading notes of Brett's ultra-licious body wash. She'd noted the brand in the bathroom. Her future husband CHAD would have to stock up.

"What do you mean?" Tori's pulse raced. Treating Brett like a genderless roommate appealed in theory, but the reality was proving a tad difficult. Which spelt bad news—nay, verging on disastrous. Unless she found a soft sort of closure with Brett Hennessy Evans over the remaining twenty-three days and nights before he returned to Sacramento, she and CHAD were doomed.

She held her breath. Tori Jarrett did not *fail*. The word wasn't in her vocabulary. She made adjustments, she reassessed if necessary, but then she avalanched ahead. Otherwise, she wouldn't get anything done. These coming weeks with Brett weren't any different.

"The living room," he responded, doling out sweet and sour pork. Rex perched at attention on the floor at their feet, black nose twitching and pink tongue hanging. "When should we install the drywall? I'm too swamped this week, but I'm free this weekend."

"Uh, John Radford is helping me, remember?" John had learned about Mick's broken collarbone Sunday morning when John and another neighbor, Clint Traymour, arrived for the carpet. Brett had been in the room when John offered. He'd heard John's every word.

"Right." Brett waggled the serving fork. "Never mind."

"I can't never mind." Tori had worked a shift at the Retro Vibe after John and Clint left. She'd returned home around six to discover Brett had sanded all the remaining moldings and baseboards. He'd accomplished a ton of appreciated but unnecessary work. "You can help when you have time, but you're not my indentured servant." And John needed to feel useful.

"Forget I asked. You must be famished." Brett held the box of sweet and sour pork beneath her nose. "Take a whiff."

She inhaled, taste buds tingling. "I could devour the whole thing." Yesterday, they had each worked long hours at their respective jobs, but today Tori had sanded every piece of door and window trim—before Brett could. Hunger gnawed her belly, and her shoulders ached like a rotten tooth.

"Remember your parents' Thursday night food fests? All the takeout I could cram into my gut. I'd starve myself for hours in anticipation."

Tori's lips quirked. By twelve, she had entered full-blown older-boy crush mode, whiling away dozens of those Thursday nights dreaming about she and Brett opening *their* home in a similar fashion to their kids' friends. Now, when ancient yearnings tugged her heartstrings, she visualized CHAD at her side. So far, the colors of her fictional future husband's eyes and hair remained hazy, although his muddled outline radiated a welcoming aura.

Yes, once she found closure with Brett, anything was possible. Love, marriage, babies. Golden anniversaries and rocking chairs.

With CHAD.

"You'd deprive yourself of food for hours?" she teased her sorority-sister-ish housemate. "Awwww."

Brett's deep chuckle wriggled beneath her skin. "I'll have you know that to a growing sixteen-year-old guy, five hours without food is a lifetime."

"How'd you ever manage to sleep?"

He winked, and her tummy swooped. "Midnight cereal binges." He carried their plates to the dining nook.

Wiping an imaginary drop of sweat from her brow—hunkadory, the guy turned her *on*—Tori stole a peek at his butt. Little glimpses were mandatory, to secure her future with CHAD. She would glimpse until Brett held zero power over her libido. She would glimpse, glimpse, glimpse, and then forget the man completely come July. And until the memory of those painful moments following their lovemaking retreated to a puny sixteenth-inch square of her heart.

But for now Brett's tan business pants draped spectacular buns. That much about the guy hadn't changed—he possessed glorious glutes. As seemed to be his habit upon arriving home from Sugartree, he'd rolled up his shirtsleeves. Golden hair burnished his muscular forearms. If memory served, whorls a half-shade darker sprinkled his broad chest and treasure-trailed below his sexy navel.

In contrast, Tori's loose tank top and track pants possessed the appeal of an over-ripe banana. At least, she'd showered after her sanding session, saving the takeout food from a sprinkling of grimy dust.

She carted chopsticks and ice-cold glasses of pink lemonade to the nook. Rex snuffled on her heels, and she shooed her pet beneath the table. Brett slid along the cushioned bench to the end space. Tori sat at the corner, Rex slobbering on her moccasins. Nudging away the dog's head, she gestured to the swinging door.

"I might remove that door and hinges. What do you think? They closed off kitchens in old houses to conceal sinks of dirty dishes and messy meal prep. I can't afford it now, but someday I want to gut the kitchen and open this entire space. Move the appliances, add an island, and create an informal family dining area. I can lose the door right away and demo the wall later."

"That's a lot of work." Brett snapped apart both pairs of chopsticks. "Essentially, you'd be installing drywall in the living room just to tear it down again."

"Only one short end of that room. The big renovation won't occur for years. In the meantime, I want my living room walls to match." And CHAD, she decided, would know his way around a nail gun. Chances were he hosted a do-it-yourself TV show.

Brett swiped the chopsticks against each other, eradicating splinters. "Judging from the exposed studs in the living room as well as the layout of the basement, the appliance wall isn't load-bearing. You'll need to check to make sure. Or ask Ry."

Tori shook her head. She wouldn't hassle her brother, who, before his divorce, worked as a project manager for his ex-father-in-law's construction firm. She, their parents, and Ry's Portland friends had promised to allow him space while he recuperated from Giselle's bombshell. That meant, except in case of emergency, not even a message to his personal webmail, which he periodically checked when in the vicinity of an Internet cafe.

"I'll ask Dad next time he and Mom call. If he doesn't know, he'll recommend someone. Until and unless Ry specifies otherwise, he's off-grid *and* off-limits." She accepted a set of chopsticks. "Thanks."

"You're welcome," Brett said. "And I get it. No bugging Ry." His gaze grew thoughtful. "You know, just brainstorming, you could remove the frame along with the door and hinges now. That would widen the opening on either side without impacting the wall or the new wiring." He dipped his chopsticks into his beef and broccoli.

"And create a cool arch?" Tori bounced on her seat. "That's perfect!"

"I hope your newbie assistant John knows what he's doing—"

"I'll google how to create the arch. They might have kits or special molding. Thanks again, Brett." Her remodeling dreams were a work in progress, designed to occur over several stages. She gazed at her houseguest from beneath lowered lashes.

Was Brett onto something? Could they become friends?

Were they a work in progress?

She glanced at her renovations planner on the far side of the nook table. If she were alone, she'd zip open that baby and jot the new ideas bubbling in her brain.

His gaze followed hers. "What's in the case?"

"Remodeling stuff." She chewed and swallowed a small mouthful of noodles. "I file receipts and invoices, notes for the work I'm doing this summer, and ideas for the future. The planner bundles everything."

His smile crooked at one corner. "Ever hear of a gadget called a computer?"

"You just revealed how little you know." She pointed her chopsticks at the planner. "That zippered edition sold out online within hours. I had to set an alarm to ensure I didn't miss the release."

"Sounds like freezing in a sleeping bag on a sidewalk for concert tickets in the olden days."

She chuckled. "My bed is more comfortable than a sleeping bag, thank you."

Heat flickered in his gaze…and radiated on her face. Tori gulped. Why for the love of God had she mentioned her bed?

Beneath the table, Rex repositioned himself. Within seconds, the beagle's rattling snores rumbled at their feet. She and Brett grinned, glancing down.

"Our meals are safe for now," Tori said.

Brett tweezered chow mein with his chopsticks. "I'll stick with my phone calendar, but a paper planner suits you. Like the Retro Vibe and your to-do lists."

"What can I say? I have a retro soul." She sipped her pink lemonade, the flavor two-stepping tart and sweet notes on her tongue. "Digital calendaring clutters my mind. Checking off tasks provides a sense of accomplishment. My colored pens feel more rewarding than my phone."

"I hear you. More tasks than you can shake a stick at pack my cell." He patted a pants pocket.

"Ever wonder about that phrase? What stick? And why would anyone want to shake it?"

"When I was little, my dad would say, 'More flies than you can shake a stick at.' I dunno, maybe in the extra-olden days, farmers shook sticks at flies to wave them off cows."

Tori moistened her lips. The Brett she remembered rarely spoke about his father. Since returning to Portland, he had mentioned Hank Evans two or three times. Visiting the old neighborhood must have stirred countless memories.

"But the cows can swish off flies with their tails," she responded in a light voice.

His eyebrows bobbled. "Maybe the farmers shook sticks at the cows so the damn bovines would get the lead out and move on to the next pasture before nightfall."

"Which brings us to the burning question of why the cows had lead in them in the first place. What the heck does 'Get the lead out' mean?"

"Face it, Tori, we're not meant to understand everything in life. Some of us aren't anyway." Brett gazed at her. "I think you've nailed it." His chopsticks rose up and down as he ate. "Your family and friends can count on you. When you make a promise, you keep it. When you care about someone, you show up. You aren't afraid to put your heart on the line." A wry sparkle lit his gaze. "I might have quoted every greeting card on the planet, but there you go."

"Oh, Brett." A sweet ache blossomed beneath her breastbone. Despite how he had hurt her four years ago, despite whatever problems existed between them now or might linger unresolved in the future, another thing that hadn't changed about Brett Evans was that he was genuinely nice.

She wished it were otherwise. She wished he were so full of himself he couldn't swallow a Rice Krispie. But this man...this sincere, if slightly clueless, software engineer...Tori didn't know how not to sympathize with his family struggles. His childhood had been so different from hers and Ryan's.

"Can I ask you something?"

"Shoot."

She rested her chopsticks on her plate. "I was too young to remember your relationship with your dad before everything... fell apart. Are you and he in contact? Do you miss him?"

A cloud passed over Brett's blue, blue eyes. "If you count receiving a birthday card during the years a girlfriend reminds him to send one—scrawled in her handwriting—we're in contact."

Tori wrinkled her nose. "That's a no."

"I miss my mom. Seeing her only at Christmas or when I travel to Florida for work is tough. I miss..." A gruff edge roughened his voice. "...the father I thought I knew before I realized he treated my mom like dirt. When you're six and your parents split, you can't comprehend what's going on, just that a parent suddenly isn't around. Whether he was there a whole lot before the divorce doesn't register until you experience how he treats you after he's out of the house."

The ache in her chest sharpened into a deep-seated pang. "I remember you saw less of him as the years passed."

His hand curled around his lemonade glass. "For a while, I thought of Hank as this cool dude dad, but then I would hang out here with Ry—" His fingers gripped the tumbler. "Even at eight or nine, I noticed your parents treated each other with kindness and consideration. That didn't mesh with what went on at my place before my mom kicked Hank out. And then..." He glanced over. "You really want to hear this?"

"Yes." She retrieved her chopsticks and pushed around a broccoli spear.

"Okay. Well, they say life has defining moments, and this was one for me." Sipping his lemonade, he shifted on the bench while Rex snuffled and snorted beneath the table. "Ry and I were ten. I sprained my thumb goofing around at softball practice. I didn't want to come off like a wuss, so the assistant coach drove me home instead of calling Mom to pick me up. She didn't expect me for another hour. I slipped inside. She was having coffee with a friend in the kitchen, and I didn't want to bug them. I decided to bandage my thumb myself. Except then I heard the lady crying about issues with her husband." Brett drew in a breath. "She asked my mom how she learned my dad was cheating on her, back when I was six. Until that day after practice, I didn't have an inkling."

Tori pressed a hand to her throat. "Brett, no! I'm sorry. That's awful. When I was a teenager, I heard your father had an affair,"—the entire neighborhood had hated Hank Evans for hurting Brett and his mom, it had seemed—"but Ryan has never said a word about that day." Or when Brett learned about his father's betrayal. At the tender age of ten.

"Your brother is a great guy, a real friend. I told him in confidence. It means a lot that he honored my trust."

Honored his trust. Unlike her, who hadn't mentioned her virginity the night of Ryan's wedding. In Brett's worldview, she'd lied by omission.

"I'm disappointed in you, Tori," had followed on the heels of, *"This was a mistake."*

Frustration burst in her chest. *Past*, she reminded herself. That night was their past. Tonight was about Brett's childhood pain, not the blunders of her over-exuberant, twenty-two-year-old self.

She nibbled a twig of sauce-drenched broccoli. "Did your mom see you?"

"Unfortunately, yes. I didn't mean to eavesdrop. I tried sneaking into my room. As I passed the kitchen, the floor squeaked, and she looked straight at me. The guilt on her face felt like dozens of magician's swords piercing a magic box. Except I was in the box, and the blades represented everything I'd thought I'd known about my father slicing me into ribbons." He released a gusty breath.

Tori remained quiet, allowing him a moment to compose himself and continue.

"It was obvious she hadn't wanted me to learn about my dad that way. I was horrified. I couldn't move. I didn't know what to do. For a second, I don't think she did either."

Tori clasped his arm. The muscles bunched beneath her touch. "You were ten, Brett. Your mom wanted you to have a good relationship with your dad. She wouldn't have said anything to poison you against him, especially at such a young age."

"I understand that." He wiped his mouth with a paper napkin. "But by then I'd started connecting the dots on my own. It wasn't Mom's fault if Hank arrived late for visitations or sometimes didn't show." His lips flattened. "Mom's friend left, apologizing the whole time. Mom talked to me while she patched my thumb. She said everything parents tell their kids about a split. That I wasn't to blame. That I shouldn't let what I'd overheard impact how I felt about my father."

"But it did," Tori murmured.

"You betcha." Brett chomped his last piece of pork. "That day marked the beginning of me coming to terms with the humiliating fact that my dad was a jackass. My parents' marriage was all about him and his needs." He muttered 'needs' like a dirty word. "Once I saw him for who he was, it began hitting me from every direction. It made it worse that he couldn't bother hiding his contempt for my mother, or for women in general. I was fourteen when he made a comment about a woman passing us on the street that pushed me over the edge." A steely glint slanted his eyes. The hurt in his voice echoed every bit as keenly.

Tori's breathing tightened. "What did he say?"

"Some crap about how the woman wasn't stacked enough to merit his attention. This was after he'd leered at her and she cringed as if he gave her the creeps. He laughed off her reaction and clapped me on the back like I was one of his drinking buddies and not an impressionable fourteen-year-old. He said only a chick with killer tits could tempt him to cheat on his current squeeze, so no loss."

Tori's mouth dropped open. "He said that? To you?" *At fourteen?*

Brett nodded. "I let him have it right there on the sidewalk in front of a little-kid candy store. I ripped into him for cheating on my mom. And do you know what he did?"

Tori wanted to cry. Brett's pain was palpable. On his face. In his voice. "What?"

"He laughed again. At me. At his son. He said Mom was 'getting saggy' when they were together, and he couldn't help it that he'd strayed."

Tori stared. She couldn't even blink. It felt like invisible toothpicks propped open her eyes. This was Brett's defining memory of his father? Puzzle pieces about his dating philosophy snapped into place. Had he constructed a code of conduct of sorts to protect his emotions and the hearts of the women who shared his dating beliefs? Like a warped system of romantic checks and balances?

His upper lip curled. "It gets better. Or worse, depending on your perspective. Hank told me having a kid with my mom was supposed to settle him down. Like my entire existence was for his benefit." His chopsticks stabbed the air. "But it didn't work. He still lusted after other women, he said. When Mom asked about receipts in his laundry, he didn't deny 'stepping out' on her. Those were his exact words. He decided he wanted what he wanted, and that was a hot young thing on his arm, not a woman with stretch marks and 'ten extra pounds of flab.' Which was how he described my mom, sniggering like the class clown while he put her down in front of a stupid candy store." Brett's chopsticks clattered onto his plate. His hands flew up and pushed outward. "I vowed then and there that I would never be like him. I like to think I've managed."

Tori permitted a trickle of air to enter her lungs. "By not allowing yourself to have real relationships?"

"They're real enough for me at this stage of my life. Each person has the same expectations. No one is pulling a fast one on the other. When one person feels emotions are becoming sticky, the situation dissolves."

"I don't know, Brett. That sounds more like a negotiation than a relationship." Like a how-to manual for not falling in love. For not risking his heart. For not living.

He shook his head. "Not everyone wants to get married and have kids. I might change my mind when I'm older. I don't know. Right now, I don't have a burning need to replicate myself, and that's okay. It should be okay not to want children. If more people gave having kids serious thought instead of treating the decision like a solution to a personal problem, maybe we wouldn't have so many unwanted, unloved children running around."

What a sad thing to believe. "Well, I'm glad you're running around. I don't think about having kids in terms of replicating myself. Children are a natural expression of a loving relationship." And exactly what she yearned for.

"And that's great for you, Tori. We're just different."

Cool pinpricks dotted her skin in the overheated kitchen. Brett's approach to life sounded lonely. He didn't have a rudder, more like a seat on a battered dinghy that sloshed from wave to wave.

"Does your dad still live in Salem?" Her moccasin nudged her dog's cuddly body beneath the table. She picked at her food with her chopsticks, selecting a morsel. "Ryan mentioned he moved back to Oregon from Alaska a couple of years ago."

"As far as I know, yeah, Hank is nearby."

"Will you see him while you're in town?" Fewer than fifty miles separated Portland from the smaller city.

"I don't expect he's changed, so why bother?"

Because it sounded like Brett needed closure with his father much in the way Tori craved a soft landing with him. She couldn't up and announce the comparison like a price checker broadcasting from a discount store loudspeaker. It was a sensitive subject. She needed to maneuver the idea into their conversation.

"How long since you last saw him?"

"Eight years. Before he moved to Alaska. He stopped by my place in Seattle for a few awkward minutes."

Around the time Brett would have graduated from college and started his first job, Tori surmised. "How did that go?

"Not well. I really don't know what he wanted, other than a quick see-you-some-year. He couldn't seem to spit it out."

Tori could hazard a guess about the reason for Hank's visit. Or was she being naive? Maybe the man had longed for Brett to forgive him. Maybe Hank had matured or regretted his behavior with his son but hadn't known how to effectively communicate his remorse. Everyone was capable of growth. Of change. Even Brett's father.

Despite that Brett was the result of an unplanned pregnancy, Sharon Evans must have seen something in Hank to become involved with him in the first place. Brett's mom was a kind, understanding, capable, and strong woman. The neighborhood rumor mill had churned out the word that Hank had taken to marriage like a convict bewildered to find himself in prison after years on the lam. Still, positive qualities might lurk beneath a coarse exterior. Some unfortunate souls remained dredged in the muck of past mistakes, unable to move forward. Lacking a plan for progress, as it were. For maximizing life's potential. Was Brett's father such a man?

A spark of hope kindled in Tori. Opportunity surrounded her temporary housemate. Brett wanted to reach a good place with her, but, with effort, might father and son also attempt to heal? Or, at the minimum, totter a few tentative steps toward building a better relationship?

"Brett." Slipping her chopsticks onto her plate, she cleared her throat. "What happened with your dad when you were fourteen was bad." Reprehensible. Emotionally scarring. "Hank shouldn't have said those things to you. No father should speak to their child that way. I'm not making excuses for him, but have you considered reaching out while you're home? Eight years is significant. It must be around sixteen years since that day outside the candy store. Hank might have done some soul-searching. He could surprise you."

A sad smile touched Brett's lips. "I doubt it." He paddled his palms on the tabletop, signifying his wish to change the subject. Lickety-split. "About the drywall. Did you speak to a supplier?"

Tori studied his hooded eyes and tense jaw. She'd better shelve the topic before she scared him off the idea of ever reconciling with his father. "The boards can be delivered with a day's notice." She reached for her planner. Her stiff muscles clenched. "Ow." Painful spasms rocked her shoulders.

Brett's hand shot to her arm. "What hurts?"

"My shoulder. Ouch. The right one." Resting her palm on the table, she carefully tipped her neck to stretch the sore muscle. Another spasm clamped down. "Ow!" She jumped out of the nook, accidentally booting Rex. The dog yelped and scampered from his napping spot. Brown ears flapped.

"Down, Rex." Brett signaled to the dog when Rex pawed her leg. "Tori, you need a massage." He slid out of the nook.

She winced. "I have an electric wand in my bedroom."

"A vibrator?"

"No!" She laughed despite the pain. "My dad's old back massager. It looks like a cute alien creature with rotating knobs instead of eyes. The problem is it's too heavy to use on my back by myself." She smiled faintly. "Whoever heard of an electric vibrator?"

"Yours has batteries?"

"We are not discussing my vibrator," she stated in a Mother Superior tone, praying he hadn't noticed she hadn't denied owning one of the pleasure-inducing devices.

"Why, Tori, I wouldn't dream of it." He rested a hand on her mid-spine. "The thing is, my buddy, my pal, you don't need a vibrator or a massage wand. You have me."

6

"TORI, RELAX," BRETT soothed his childhood friend from his spot behind the low-backed living room sofa. She sat on the couch with her gaze pinned to the wall separating the large space from the kitchen, her posture stiff as a gargoyle looming from the rooftop of a medieval cathedral.

"Where's Rex?" Her voice squeaked and her muscles twitched —and Brett had yet to touch her.

Slowly, he settled his palms on her cement-sack trapezoids. The warmth of her skin created an almost-palpable humming sensation against the pads of his fingers. "Your dog went outside," he uttered through a tight throat.

Ryan's little sister, Ryan's little sister. He repeated the mantra over and over.

"I didn't hear the pet door."

"Because you're in pain." The beagle had chosen a fine time to explore the backyard. Just when Brett apparently required a chaperone. Where was Mini-Val now, huh? Definitely not hovering near his ear issuing terse rejoinders.

Both Val and Rex had abandoned Brett to the enticement of a pink bra strap slipping out from Tori's blue tank top, which she wore tucked haphazardly into baggy track pants. As if she didn't give a rip about her appearance.

Baggy track pants. Slapdash tucking. *Ryan's sister, Ryan's sister.* Baggy and slapdash and not at all attractive to a socially awkward computer nerd.

Brett had drawn a line in the sand with the friendship issue, and he intended to honor it. He had accomplished the task easily enough throughout his adolescence and young adulthood. Years before Tori's brother's wedding, Brett visited Ryan during a weekend home from college. He recalled Tori exiting the basement workshop, where she had been helping her dad. Brett had caught her twinkling gaze in the seconds before she ducked into the rec room bathroom, her smile chipper and her sassy rear rounding out her jeans.

Not a split-second later, Ry made it abundantly clear that Brett had looked a little too long.

Ryan punched Brett's shoulder. "Why are you staring at my sister, dude?"

"I'm not." Brett snorted. "She looks different. Her hair is inches from her waist." And, at fifteen, she was developing curves on curves. But Brett wouldn't point out the obvious.

"Yeah, she's growing up," Ry said. "So keep your eyes focused elsewhere."

"I don't think about Tori like that!"

"And you never will."

After that awkward episode, Brett had exerted extreme diligence to never again look at Tori in anything other than a brotherly fashion. The night of Ryan's wedding, his self-restraint shattered.

That had been unacceptable.

He now realized that to a twenty-two-year-old Tori, their tumble in bed had symbolized a promise for the future. *Them.* Together. Perhaps for all time.

But what did he know about commitment? Or marriage? The

rancid sludge of Hank's blood oozed in his veins. DNA packed a mighty wallop. He was better off alone.

Tori popped up from the sofa. "Should I check on Rex?"

"What? Who? No." Tapping her arm, Brett encouraged her to sink onto the couch. "Your dog is on sniff patrol. He loves it. I checked the fence the other day and didn't notice any broken boards."

"Dad was single-minded about repairing loose slats when Rex was a puppy. Beagles are escape artists."

"So the yard is secure. The hound is having fun." Rex preferred his snout gliding along the ground vacuum-cleaner fashion.

"I suppose you're right." Tori scratched her scalp. Then clasped her fidgety hands on her lap. One lurched out to rub a knee. She gripped her fingers tighter. Her right thumb squeezed the left until the nail glowed red.

"If you keep that up, you'll snap a joint."

Her hands loosened a smidgen.

Gently, Brett pressed the fleshy bases of his palms into her knotted shoulders. "Those boulders in there?" he asked, basking in the warmth of her responding, if jittery, laughter. "Close your eyes," he coached. Exactly like a coach. Like his childhood softball coach or Stan Weldon the high school football coach he'd encountered five days ago in the Retro Vibe. He smiled. Now he was in the groove. "If it doesn't hurt too much, let your head hang forward."

Tori followed his advice. A wince drifted to Brett's ears. An agonized sigh trailed behind.

He parted Tori's silky hair, revealing the sore curve of her neck. She flinched. The poor girl was hurting bad.

Maintaining a light touch, he plied her shoulders. Within moments, her bunched muscles yielded, softening beneath his hands. A quiet moan toppled from her lips.

Gritting his teeth against the subtle sensuality shimmering in the innocent sound, he lowered his head. "How's that?" His jaw brushed the hair covering her ear. "Do you need less pressure? Or more?"

"Oh, Brett," she whispered, voice feathery. "How you're doing it…really hurts. But also feels like heaven, if that makes sense."

Not quite. Heaven was in her arms, buried deep in her body.

Sucking in air, he snapped upright. He needed to watch himself. A year had passed since his last relationship, a side effect of his hectic schedule. Right now, massaging a lamppost would light his fire. Sooner or later, he would grow immune to the undeniable chemistry he shared with his best friend's sister. For now, a well-timed visit to his favorite topic was in order.

"Back to the drywall." He stared at the coffee table, willing a specific body part to remain as immobile as humanly possible. "Are you happy with your supplier?"

Tori's head shifted up and down in an infinitesimal nod. Her curtain of brown-sugar hair shielded her expression. "Dad's contact from his hardware days quoted an excellent price. Everything is under control."

Unlike Brett's imagination. "Okay." Tori was the most capable female he knew, not only when it came to her house renovations but also in the management of the Retro Vibe. He couldn't sloth about her home while she remodeled it around him. He wasn't built that way. "Which project should we tackle first? Installing the drywall or refinishing the floor?"

"Huh?" Her head tilted to one side. Brett's fingers grazed the velvet skin bordering her exposed bra strap. "Can you repeat that?" she whispered languidly. "I'm a little involved in what you're doing to my back."

He chuckled. "If we put up the drywall first,"—which necessitated mudding, sanding, and usually painting—"the dust from refinishing the floors will ruin the new paint." The soles of his wingtips scraped the worn oak. "I'm thinking we should sand the floors before slapping on the new wallboards."

"I considered the same thing," Tori replied in a mellow tone. "But when I refinish the floors, I don't want to restrict myself to the living room and hall. The bedrooms need updating too. I'll work on—oh, that's a good spot. Yes, *there*." She moaned. "I'll put up the walls now. Around August, once you're not here anymore, Rex and I can stay with Val while Ry helps refinish the floors. The paint will have cured by then, and Rex will be safe in Val's chain-linked yard. It's like a little doggy jail."

A frown yanked down the corners of Brett's mouth. "I didn't realize my moving in would impact your schedule." He wanted to help—not hinder—her momentum. "Why didn't you say something?" He massaged a stubborn knot, fingers grinding against the ribbed fabric of her tank top.

"No, no, don't worry about it. Oh...ahhh...that hurts so good." Her head tipped the other direction. She released a low groan. "It didn't occur to me to refinish the bedroom floors until after I asked you to stay. A sander with a dust bag attachment will do double duty toward protecting the new paint. It's not a problem."

Another groan drifted from her lowered head. Brett yearned to part the glossy strands. To cup her face and—

Stop it. What a pig he was. This was Tori. Thoroughly and irresistibly sexy but—

Tori, man. Shake it off.

"Yes," she whispered as his fingers brushed a bra strap. "Right...under there. If you don't mind?"

His hands stilled. "Under"—he hooked a finger beneath the left strap—"here?" Was she trying to torture him?

She nodded. "Slide the strap off my shoulder and...and slip your hand beneath my top. Um, through the armhole might work best."

Say what? "Not from under the hem?"

"Correct. Don't ..." She inhaled. "...lift my shirt. Just go through the hole."

Go through the hole. "Got it." He hoped he sounded normal.

"And Brett? Can you slide off both straps?"

A fog of lust misted his brain. "Are you having a spasm?"

"Yes. Can't you feel it?" Her muscles jumped beneath the straps.

"I can now." She was in a world of pain.

Humming a radio jingle, he edged down the bra straps until they ensnared her upper arms. Visualizing his mother dismembering a raw chicken, he slipped his hands into the stretchy armholes of Tori's sleeveless shirt. Tiny goosebumps pebbled her flesh. Her shoulders wriggled as he rested his fingers on the ridge of her shoulders and dug his thumbs into the knots lumped on either side of her spine.

"Like this?"

"Ohhh," she groaned. "Yes."

Brett concentrated on applying pressure where she most needed it. Barely audible sighs conveyed he provided relief from her renovation-induced aches. Finally, she released a long breath and leaned back against the couch—trapping his hands between her spine and the cushion. His wrists bent at an awkward angle.

He jiggled his captured hands. "Tori?"

Her eyelids drifted open. The honeyed hazel of her irises focused on his face. "Can you massage the front of my shoulders?" she half-whispered, straightening enough to allow him to shuffle his hands free of the tank top's armholes. "Around my collarbones." Her gaze skipped about the living room, as if seeking an anchor and finding none. "I hurt everywhere." Her eyes fell shut as she sagged against the sofa cushion. Her lashes settled like delicate crescents against her creamy skin.

Brett gazed at her parted mouth and full, pink lips. The devil must be dancing in hell tonight, because this massage was a Herculean test of his fortitude.

He slipped his fingers beneath the neckline of her top. His fingertips sat on the tense muscles below her collarbone, where her breasts swelled upward. Propping his thumbs on her shoulders, he rolled his fingertips on her tight muscles in slow, circular motions.

"Ohhh," she murmured. "You have the magic touch."

Brett concentrated on providing clinical relief. His thumb bumped a lump the size of three frozen peas. He circled the knot with his fingers. "The right side feels tighter."

"Work on the left as well. Just don't stop. Please don't stop."

He cocked an eyebrow. Where had he heard those words before?

Purely out of a kind of medical curiosity, he peeked at her closed eyes and upturned face. The rosy glow dusting her skin brought to mind the beautiful flush on her cheeks in the aftermath of their long-ago lovemaking.

Her breathing grew shallow. "B-Brett? The middle of my back is really sore. Can you sit behind me and...?"

"Massage it?"

Her eyes opened. "Yes, please." She pushed the coffee table farther from the couch, arranged her knees to the side, and turned half-away on the cushion. Her hand reached around her back. She indicated the area of her bra clasp with her thumb. "The ache is under here."

Brett's tongue poked the inside of his cheek. Was she serious?

"I can unhook my bra and—" She glanced over her shoulder. "Why are you camped out behind the couch?"

Because he required a barricade. "I can't undo your bra, Tori."

"You don't have to. My muscles feel much looser now." She blinked. "I'll unfasten the clasp. Sorry. Didn't I say that?"

Her muscles might feel loose, but his—including one over which he possessed zero control—jerked and twitched and stiffened.

"You can't undo your bra either."

Flicking a hand, she stood. "You're a guy. You wouldn't know. There's a simple trick. I'll show you." She pushed her hands up the back of her top. With a yank here and a twist there, she unclasped the hook and scooped the bra out an armhole. The pink lingerie tumbled onto the coffee table. Her unrestricted breasts bounced beneath the ribbed garment.

Brett's 'muscle' saluted his zipper.

He scraped a palm along his cheek. *Oh, no. Oh, no, no.* This wouldn't do.

"I wasn't referring to your ability to undo your bra. I'm concerned about appropriate behavior."

A tiny furrow etched between her eyebrows.

"Behavior, Tori. Between pals. We established boundaries."

She scoffed. "You're the one with boundaries, Evans. Confined and squished and imprisoned in a tidy box." Her hands pantomimed constructing a cube. Her breasts bounced along with the rapid motions of her fingers. He couldn't think when her breasts bounced. "I'm well aware we are pals, Brett." Her voice rang. "You don't need to keep reminding me."

"Evidently, I do."

Her nostrils flared. "A pal wouldn't offer a dream massage and then stop the moment his friend is feeling better."

A pal would do exactly that.

"Do you have a lot of experience massaging pals?"

She tossed her head. Her glorious hair flounced around her shoulders. "Meridy and I gave each other massages twice a month."

He couldn't think about Tori and Meridy and massages!

"Complete with pillow fights?" he asked even as he realized this turn of conversation might as well shove him barefoot along a path of blistering coals.

She propped a hand on her hip. More bouncing ensued. "I say massages and your brain jet planes to pillow fights?" She crossed her arms beneath her breasts. The bouncing ceased, but lush cleavage plumped the neckline of her shirt. "You wanted to be pals? This is me being a pal. Girl pals give each other massages."

"Well, guy pals don't."

"You suggested a massage!"

"That was a mistake."

Red splotches sprang up in stark relief on her face. "Sort of like our night together. How you, Evans. You go along with things. You suggest solutions. Then you call off the whole shebang."

His heart raced. "That wasn't what I meant." Dub him a pessimist, but if she booted him out of her house again, he might not find another route back in. He grasped for a shred of practicality. Of reason. "A pal would discuss John." Her out-of-work neighbor.

"John? That's a leap."

It wasn't a leap. It was a lifeline. Brett grabbed the invisible rope and hung on. "Nothing against the guy, but you refused to let me pay room and board, so I'm working off my debt like we agreed. If John helps, it negates the concept."

Her eyes rounded. "*This* is the conversation you want to have now?" She pointed at the floor. Rex trucked in from the kitchen, stretched his maw, and noisily yawned.

"Yes," Brett croaked. He needed any conversation other than the one begun the instant Tori David-Copperfielded her bra.

She threw her hands in the air. More infernal bouncing occurred. Her voice rose. "Between your consulting job and the hours of work you've put in on the house so far, you must be exhausted! Don't you want time off?"

"If you don't need a break, neither do I," he shouted back. "I'm your primary helper, Tori. I'll trade in my rental car for a truck to carry the boards. Save you the cost of delivery."

"Why are you yelling?"

"Why are you?"

Her hands shot up on either side of her face. "Because." Her fingers clenched. "You're grasping at straws. And you don't make sense!"

"I make perfect sense." Didn't he?

She inhaled with the force of a small but mighty tugboat. Her lips formed the numbers, *One, two, three.*

Four.

Five.

Six, seven, eight.

"All right," she muttered through gritted teeth. Her dog sank onto the hardwood and licked his paws. "We need to reach a resolution. I can't go on like this."

What did she mean? "Go on like—?"

"How about if John delivers the boards and you help me install them?" she interrupted, waving a hand in her annoyed-with-men, insect-swatting manner.

What was it with this John guy? Why did she feel responsible for his mental health?

"It's important to you that John feels useful, isn't it?" That sounded like Brett's kindhearted friend. His Tori. When she wasn't acting bat-crap crazy.

"Yes!" She pumped two fists, excitement at his understanding lighting her eyes. "John is twiddling his thumbs hanging around their house. Letting him help me helps him."

"Understood." Brett preferred happily married John as an assistant miles ahead of twerpy Mick Seifert, considering the college kid's clumsiness and resulting injury. "John can pick up the drywall boards," he said magnanimously. John reminded him of a domesticated Labrador. A bit eager to please, but earnest and competent. And strong. "This weekend, he and I will install them. You can supervise. Nothing else. Let me do this for you." *Allow me to feel useful too.* To contribute.

In his mind, Tori's life resembled one of those species of trees connected by an immense system of roots. Each appeared independent but relied on and thrived because of the colony. What must that sense of community feel like? Would Brett ever experience a similar feeling of inclusion?

Tori's gaze considered his for another three seconds. "I'm glad we got that straightened out." She motioned at Rex. The dog's whiskers perked. "Thanks for the massage, pal," she directed at Brett. Pooch and owner turned to the hall outside the bedrooms. "I feel loads better. But, yeesh, I'm bushed. Goodnight."

The master bedroom door banged shut, corralling Tori, the dog, her indignation, and her bouncing breasts inside.

Tori collapsed against the bedroom door. The nerve of Brett Hennessy Evans! He insisted on reading sexual undertones into their every encounter or the most innocuous conversation—despite his numerous declarations that he wanted to be buddies or pals or whatever the heck he thought he wanted. Treating him like one of the girls wasn't working.

She raked her hands through her dirty hair, willing her pulse to slow. Her gaze tracked Rex circling on his doggy bed near the far nightstand. Breathing deeply, she recalled the stages of the massage. In retrospect, maybe she had crossed the line asking Brett to knead her mid-back. But could she help it if knots clumped the muscles directly beneath her bra strap, an area he'd avoided during his ministrations? Even now, the area throbbed with pain. Her spine and neck and collarbone felt wonderful. The tension from her day of sanding had evaporated beneath his talented hands, except for smack-dab below her shoulder blades.

A male masseuse wouldn't have hesitated to fulfill her request. Meridy would have unclasped the bra herself. But Brett wasn't a professional. And he definitely wasn't Meridy.

In the midst of Tori's discomfort, she might have asked too much of the poor guy. Her face warmed. Enough feeling sorry for him. What was his problem?

She pushed off the door. Didn't he realize how difficult it had been for her to agree to the massage in the first place? To endure the sensual memories that inundated her mind when he'd touched her? To center her energy on not becoming aroused for several relief-providing, although annoyingly pleasurable, minutes only for him to leave her the rubdown equivalent of high and dry?

She yanked off her tank and tossed it into an overflowing laundry basket. This was her house, and he wanted to dictate the rules. Like a father lecturing an out-of-control teenager.

She chewed the inside of her cheek, pondering those last thoughts. This was her house. She was in charge. She created the rules. And they were about to change. Whenever she damn well felt like it. She didn't do Brett's bidding. He did hers.

Snickering, she cracked open the door.

"Brett, would you be a pal and freshen Rex's outside water? Also, close the flap on the doggy door and put the leftover Chinese food in the fridge. First, buddy, can you bring me my bra?"

Brett stood motionless behind the couch. "What was that?" He cocked an ear toward the bedroom hallway. "I didn't quite catch what you said." It had been a long list of requests. And completely unanticipated. He hadn't expected to bump into Tori again until morning. If then.

Her voice snaked out of the inched-open bedroom door. "My bra."

Yep. She had really asked that.

"I'm collecting laundry before I sack out. Bring it here, okay?"

"Um, no problem." Nothing to this. It wasn't underwear. It was laundry.

Moving to the coffee table, he gripped a shoulder strap. His fingertips tingled.

He zeroed his attention on a blotchy stain on a pink cup.

Perspiration acquired over a day of intense labor but sweat just the same. Unattractive. He pulled a face. Kind of gross.

But real, another part of his mind asserted. Tori was a genuine, caring woman with family and community connections. A hard worker who earned authentic pit stains, which appeared to have smeared onto her bra cup. Not like the sophisticated women he dated.

Definitely gross.

Feeling like a tight rope walker balancing twenty stories above a street teeming with traffic, he picked his way to the bedroom hall. Tori's arm skated out between the jamb and door. Her fingers wiggled.

"Hurry up," she said, face and body hidden. "I'm busy."

Her voice sounded weird. "Doing what?"

"Laundry." Her fingers snapped. "Now." A second passed. "Chump."

Brett's chin snapped up. Was she channeling Val?

"This ain't the army, kid," he teased. "You can't order me around."

Her hand wagged. "Brett. My house. My bra. Hand it over."

Her house? What did that mean?

He held out the bra. Her fingers grazed a cup. He jerked back his hand, and the silky fabric slithered from her grasp.

"Brett!" Her right eye appeared in the opening. The iris sparkled.

"Think I'm your minion?" Brett joked as if they were kids jostling for the last piece of pizza. Except, instead of waving around a slice, he dangled the bra beyond her reach. Her fingers brushed a strap. He snatched the lingerie in his fist, mimicking her voice. "'Water my dog, Brett. Clean the kitchen, Brett. Bring my laundry.' Arf, arf. Woof."

She laughed at his imitation of a bark. "Shh, you'll wake Rex." Her arm reached again. "Give me my bra."

Brett grinned. "Say please."

The door creaked. Her hand lunged. "Give it!"

"Not a quick learner. Now you'll have to say pretty please."

Her gaze disappeared from the opening. Silence mushroomed. He could feel her thinking. Which usually spelled trouble.

With a sudden whisk, the door swung six inches wide. "Pretty"—a bare breast flashed, the nipple puckering—"please."

Brett stared. Bare breast? When had she—?

She grabbed the bra and banged the door in his face.

He scrubbed his forehead. Tori's breast. Her *naked* breast. He had caught a glimpse of his fantasies. But not his reality. Never again.

The door slid open. Tori beamed a smile through the sliver of space. "Thanks, pal." The door closed.

The sound of her movements carried from inside the room. Dresser drawers scraped as she hummed a song about girls running the world. She murmured a few bars, evidently immersed in gathering her laundry and preparing for bed. For a deep and contented sleep following a long day of toiling on her house.

Brett glanced down at the ridge straining his pants. Looked like he would be pitching tents the rest of the night.

ori's To-Do List ~ Saturday

- *Put up drywall*
- *Check propane tank for barbecue*
- *Brainstorm seducing Brett*

TORI PLACED THE covered bowl of Lorelei's pasta salad in the refrigerator. Lorelei, arms folded casually over her aquamarine sundress, kept an eye on two bubbly six-year-olds playing with Rex beneath the maple and chestnut trees. Loud hammering boomed from the front of the house, hurting Tori's ears and likely her guest's as well. In preparation for devising an arch between the living room and kitchen, the swinging door no longer separated the spaces. Brett and John attacked the installation of the drywall as if competing in a world-championship event.

"Should we enjoy our iced tea in the backyard so you can watch Daisy and her friend?" Tori asked the slim blonde looking out the kitchen window.

"That sounds nice." Lorelei glanced over, covering an ear with one hand. "What can I take out?"

"Not a thing." Tori lifted her voice above the banging. "You made the food. The least I can do is serve." And command the grill. "Go ahead. Prop open the door. I'll be right there."

Lorelei fluttered her fingers in a see-you-soon gesture. Muggy heat oozed into the over-warm house as the woman departed. Rex's excited barks and the girls' tinkling laughter floated close behind.

Tori retrieved two clear plastic jugs from the fridge. Lemon slices floated on iced tea in one. Cherry juice brimmed the other. The pitchers represented her measly contribution to the late afternoon meal. Well, and she'd raced to a convenience store for hot dogs and ice cream for the girls. Big whoop. Around noon, when Lorelei called suggesting they barbecue blue cheese hamburgers after the men finished the drywall, Tori had readily agreed. She hadn't expected her friend of fewer than seven weeks to proclaim a pasta salad, burger patties, and a tasty-sounding bacon-dip appetizer already prepared.

Tori set the full pitchers on the counter. She collected tumblers, napkins, and a large serving tray. The Radfords, living three houses away, were nice people. She'd planned to ask them to dinner before now, but the renovations had kept her hopping. And then...she wrinkled her nose...Brett happened.

Showing up on her doorstep. Waltzing into her house as if he owned the place.

Messing with her head.

The thunderous hammering continued on the opposite side of the appliance wall. The men's jocular voices echoed in the largely empty front room as John told a corny gag and Brett replied with a goofy riddle. The kind of jokes the girls could walk in on.

Dad jokes.

The two men worked well together. But, honestly, throughout the day Brett had treated John like a lifelong buddy instead of someone he had met last week. Brett's over-the-top friendliness toward Tori's neighbor was a fraction of a millimeter away from triggering the wrath of her ornery alter ego.

Never mind that she wanted John to feel useful. And that Brett's positive demeanor helped. Mr. Brett "I'm Your Pal" Evans was driving her around the bend. She felt like she'd awoken from a hazy dream to discover herself buckled into a seat on a bullet train barreling toward Frustration Town. Somehow she'd managed to purchase a nonrefundable ticket to a B movie—in totally unnecessary 3-D.

She plunked a pitcher onto the tray. Cherry juice sloshed over the rim. Her face heated. Damn it, there was no end to cherry references in her life lately. And zero solutions to her predicament with the man who'd plucked hers.

Four days ago, at her bedroom door, she'd flashed a boob at Brett. On impulse. Just to see what he would do. To teach him a lesson. To prove she was in charge.

Her spontaneous peep show had proven a monumental flop. In the intervening days, he hadn't once mentioned the incident. He'd behaved like it hadn't happened. At all.

The day after the boob flash, she'd made a production of carrying her laundry up from the basement, the freshly washed bra strewn atop her folded clothes. She'd declared the facilities available for his use. She had even included some gratuitous repositioning of the laundry basket so the bra displayed in his direct line of sight.

And how had he responded? With a banal, *"Thanks. I might do a load tomorrow."*

Her bra had practically stared him in the face, and he *might* do a load tomorrow?

Every morning he headed to work early and returned home late. They hadn't shared another meal or exchanged more than a polite, "Hey, how are you?" and "Great"—*nope*—"You?"

They might as well be strangers passing in an apartment-building hallway. Except Tori had never experienced sexual energy frizzling between herself and another tenant in the complex she'd lived in with Meridy. With Brett, attraction sparked whenever they occupied the same room.

She didn't know what she'd expected from her spontaneous game of Peek-a-Boob. A reaction of some sort. So then now what was she to think?

Either she hadn't flashed Brett properly—was there a wrong way to flash a guy?—or she'd misinterpreted his I'm-interested-but-pretending-I'm-not vibes.

Was it asking too much that she yearned to feel comfortable in her own skin? For Brett to admit he saw her as a woman and not the dreaded 'little sis'?

That they might do something about it? To work through their attraction so they could both put the past behind them?

He might be happy stagnating as pals for the duration of his stay, but gooey quicksand pulled at her ankles, threatening to suck her under.

The need for forward momentum itched beneath her skin. Where did she go from here? What logically followed a failed boob-flashing?

Squaring her shoulders, she carted the refreshment tray onto the porch and nudged shut the door with a sneakered foot. Earlier, she and Brett had arranged the patio set in the middle of the back lawn. As Tori approached the table, Lorelei wound up the umbrella. Tori slid the tray onto the tempered glass.

Lorelei smiled in the withering heat. "Thanks a bunch, Tori." She called to the children. "Daisy! Jenny! Tori made juice."

Daisy's blond curls bounced as the little girl threw Rex's ball in a wobbly arc. "We're playing, Mommy!" The dog leapt and caught the toy in his mouth. The girls squealed with delight. Rex dropped the ball at Jenny's feet. The dark-haired girl tossed it toward an overgrown carrot patch in a corner of the rear fence. The children raced after Rex.

Lorelei sank onto a patio chair and hollered. "When you're thirsty then, munchkins."

Tori filled their glasses and topped up two with juice for the girls. "Gosh, it's muggy." She spied thunderheads gathering in the gray-streaked sky. "It might storm tonight."

"I hope so." Lorelei plucked the skirt of her sundress. "We need the rain. It's too dry." She fanned a paper napkin in front of her face. Glancing toward the children, she mumbled, "If I wanted to live in hotter-than-hell, I'd move to Texas. Know what I mean?"

Tori nodded. "Or California." Where Brett lived.

Yi-yi, she had to move on.

Banishing Brett thoughts, she sat next to Lorelei. Their backs to the house, she asked, "How is John's job search going?" He was a heavy equipment mechanic. It shouldn't be long before he found employment again.

"Not too bad." Lorelei sipped her iced tea. "The poor guy. He hates not working. Oh, he's happy being available for Daisy after school, and he's been wonderful about taking on household chores now that I'm working fulltime. But for a man usually up to his elbows in grease, mopping floors and trying to cook"— Lorelei winked—"doesn't cut it."

Tori laughed. "I prefer mopping to vacuuming." The basement required carpet for warmth in the winter, although she planned to research other options. While linoleum covered the kitchen and main-floor bathroom, eventually tile would replace the dated flooring her parents chose the last time they redecorated.

A soft light entered Lorelei's eyes. "I love cooking and baking, making a home. Granted, mopping floors isn't a favorite, but I don't mind it." She paused. "John is a man's man, and I adore that about him. I don't bring in enough cash from my job at the craft store to make much difference when he's working fulltime. I get along with the staff and customers, but being a stay-at-home mom is my dream. At least, until Daisy is a teenager. John likes being the primary breadwinner, and I'm a way better cook." Her hand rested on Tori's forearm. "Thanks for asking for his help mudding the drywall when Daisy's in school. It fills him with purpose."

"You're welcome. But he's doing me the favor." Tori sipped her drink. A refreshingly chilly ice cube bumped her lips.

Lorelei leaned an elbow on the arm of her chair. "He has an interview with the city coming up. Cross your fingers he gets the job. His last employer went bankrupt two weeks after we moved into this neighborhood." A pensive note entered her voice. "Our first house that isn't a rental."

"I'm sorry, Lorelei. I wasn't aware of the details."

"I feel bad for the owners but, for us, the timing was awful." Lorelei glanced in her daughter's direction. A mysterious smile touched her lips.

"What are you thinking about?"

The woman's hand settled on her trim stomach. "Just the things John does for Daisy and me. He's such a sweet guy." A wide smile blossomed on her face. "For instance, Daisy's teacher assigned her to bring cookies to the year-end class party. I thought I would bake them rather than resorting to store-bought, but John has a family recipe passed down from his mom. This big hulk of a man keeps practicing the most disgusting chocolate chip cookie recipe I've ever tasted." Lorelei's soft laughter chimed in the muggy heat. "I'm certain my dear, departed mother-in-law miswrote the ingredients on the card, but John won't let me look at it. The cookies are dry as dust, but he won't give up. No googling or You-Tubing for my guy. He says he stood beside his mom dozens of times as a kid, waiting to lick the beaters. He's determined to conquer the ingredient list."

Tori laughed along with her neighbor. That a burly fellow like John Radford cared so much about perfecting a botched recipe for his daughter's class touched her.

Her gaze drifted to Daisy and Jenny building a house of twigs beneath a large maple while Rex dug in the unkempt carrot patch. At six, the same age as these two little girls, Tori had snuck out one summer night to follow Ry and Brett on a secret mission to filch strawberries from their then-next-door-neighbor's prized fruit and vegetable garden. The garden was huge, encompassing half of Elroy Timberton's backyard. Ry and Brett hadn't cared two flips about getting caught. They'd heard at school that trespassers were put to work weeding, which meant more opportunities to gobble fruit.

Neither boy noticed Tori in the shadows. She tripped on a rake leaning against Mr. Timberton's shed, scraping her knees. Her bawling alerted Elroy, and he caught the trio but only assigned weeding detail to Brett and Ryan. The old man bandaged Tori's wounds, gave her two dollars—one for each captured thief, he said—and sent her home with a bowl of strawberries picked fresh that morning. Ry and Brett whined big time.

The boys weeded an hour every day for a week that summer as penance. In the end, Elroy paid them and Tori received a second bowl of berries. She happily shared.

She'd worshipped Brett in those days. How had he viewed her? As a keyed-up puppy? A human version of Rex?

She continued watching the girls. A hollow sensation pinged in her chest. Would Brett become another lonely Elroy Timberton, never marrying or having children, setting out rakes as traps and commandeering a fruit-hungry team of helpers he later paid and encouraged to return whenever they needed to earn a few bucks? The other night, Brett said he didn't want kids—that he might never want a family—yet when he met Daisy and Jenny today he'd ruffled each girl's hair and told a knock-knock joke as if it were second nature.

Biting her lip, Tori looked at Lorelei. "What will you do about the cookies?"

"Wake up early the day of the party and bake a batch of my recipe to replace John's. I'll smuggle a container to the teacher before work. She and I have discussed it. If I time it right, John won't suspect and his ego will survive."

"Won't he smell them baking?"

"He sleeps like a log. The key is dragging myself out of bed before dawn. I tire easily." Her hand moved on her midsection.

Tori's eyes widened. "You're not—?" She directed her gaze to Lorelei's flat stomach.

"Pregnant?" the woman whispered. She nodded. "I just found out."

Tori whispered back, "Congratulations."

"I'm nine weeks along." Lorelei's eyes cut to Daisy and Jenny running toward the table. Lorelei put down her glass and handed juice to each child. The girls gulped their drinks. Red liquid dribbled off Daisy's lips.

"Sweetie, what was I thinking dressing you in white?" Lorelei wiped a napkin over her daughter's mouth. Jenny stuck out her chin, and Lorelei rubbed an invisible spot.

Rex bolted to a water bowl near the table. The girls set down their glasses and crouched, chattering to the bright-eyed dog.

"John doesn't know yet," Lorelei whispered behind a curved hand. "I don't want him stressing about another mouth to feed. We figured this one"—she angled her head toward Daisy —"would be our only." A fine sheen of tears glistened on her eyes. "I *am* happy."

Tori's heart turned over. "Lorelei, tell him. You need his support."

"I'll break the news soon. Hopefully, after he gets that job. Then we can celebrate properly instead of him worrying I'm working too hard."

Rex abandoned the water bowl. Sniffing the grass in giant figure eights, he meandered back to the carrot patch. Each girl marched solemnly behind the beagle—two loyal subjects serving at the pleasure of His Royal Rexness.

"All I've ever wanted is to be a good wife and mother," Lorelei said as the girls wandered out of earshot. "At thirty-two and with my fertility problems, no way did I think this would happen now."

Tori passed her cool glass to her other hand. Lorelei's love for her husband and family radiated on her face and in her voice. Would she ever experience such depth of emotion with a man?

Cory had wanted kids. CHAD would. Obviously, or he wouldn't be CHAD. Her Caring, Honest, Attractive, Dad-material future husband.

First, she needed to meet the guy.

"I was twenty-six when we had Daisy," Lorelei went on. "I would've preferred a shorter gap between babies, but at this point,"—she lifted her glass in a toast—"hurrah!"

They clinked glasses.

"I'm twenty-six now." Tori stared into her iced tea. Brett's reappearance was a temporary stumbling block along the way to meeting CHAD. Of this, she was well aware. Except, when confronted with the loving routine the Radfords shared, her world of work, friends, and community sports suddenly felt like she was biding time. This year, because of the house and also because she and Cory had divided their teams according to who had joined a league first, she hadn't even participated in mixed softball.

"Some women wait until their forties to have kids," Lorelei commented. "It's more important to find the right guy." She studied Tori. "I've watched friends leap into bad relationships because they glimpse thirty on the horizon. Don't make that mistake. When the perfect man comes along, you'll know."

"That's what I keep telling myself." Four years ago, she'd found the perfect guy. In Brett. Or so she'd thought.

Lorelei read her mind. "Brett is great."

"Uh, *no*." Tori stuck to the script. "He's my brother's best friend, almost like a big brother to me." *Liar, liar, pants on fire.* "He lived in the neighborhood years ago. Across the alley and four doors down."

"Hmm." Lorelei's gaze pinned Tori in place. "Love can grow from friendship."

"Love can destroy it too." To hear Brett talk.

She directed her attention to the girls and Rex. Daisy and Jenny collapsed on their backs, arms and legs sweeping the grass. Rex licked Daisy's arm. Little-girl giggles lifted into the hot air.

"Lord, that dress," Lorelei murmured but didn't disrupt her daughter's play.

Tori looked back at her friend. "Lorelei, why don't I bake the cookies for Daisy's party? You have enough to deal with. It will be easier to fool John if I do it."

"Tori, would you? But you're crazy busy."

"Maybe, but this is empty." Tori pointed to her womb. A poignant ache squeezed her insides. "Which day is the party?"

The sound of the kitchen door opening and closing reverberated from the porch. "Here come the guys," Lorelei said beneath her breath. "I'll text you."

Pasting on a smile, Tori tossed a quick glance over her shoulder. John, a giant of a man at around six-four with thinning sandy hair and a tad too much love happening around the middle, strode onto the lawn alongside Brett. Sweat soaked their T-shirts and glistened on their forearms. They grinned like construction workers off to meet hot babes after work.

Tori's stomach tightened. She wanted to be Brett's hot babe, damn it. Even if only for a short time. Despite realizing they had no future.

Lorelei greeted the guys, caressing her husband's lower back. John kissed his wife. Daisy ran over and leapt into his arms.

"Daddy!"

"Hi, Squirt." John nuzzled Daisy's neck. Jenny and Rex scampered to the table. "Hey, Jenny." He looked at Lorelei and Tori. "You ladies ready for some grub?"

Lorelei pinched her nose. "Wash first?"

John laughed. "You don't approve of my studly aroma?" He kissed Daisy's temple. The girl squirmed, squeezing her nose in imitation of her mom. "I'll pop home, clean up, and bring back a cold six-pack. Sound good, Brett?"

"Thanks, man. I'll jump in the shower. If you don't mind, Tori?"

A yummy visual of her housemate shedding his clothes invaded her gray matter. In her fantasies, Hornery Tori quipped, *"Want company?"*

Her real self, on script, kept her lips zipped.

Hours after the Radfords left, Brett lounged on the rec room couch, Rex snoring on a blanket below his sock-covered feet. On Ry's wide-screen, bullets pierced bodies and fists crunched jaws as hitmen pulverized every target within sight. Meanwhile, Tori soaked in her birthday suit in a hot bath on the main floor above Brett and her snoozing hound. The action movie was supposed to have distracted Brett from the categorically non-platonic images whipping through his depraved imagination. The Bra Incident had tortured him for days. Memories of a dewy-eyed, ultra-responsive Tori on her brother's wedding night gushed unnecessary fuel onto his agonizing fire.

Following the departure of their late-afternoon dinner guests, Tori had set about staining baseboards in the workshop. Brett had taken advantage of her self-imposed exile to fiddle with the arch kit in the kitchen, in preparation for installation tomorrow. Throughout the day, they'd interacted with the Radfords while awkwardly avoiding each other. How long before the situation normalized?

Would conditions normalize?

The back of his neck tingled. He couldn't shake the niggling sensation that his hostess had allowed the bedroom door to swing too wide on purpose Tuesday night. Enough for him to catch a glimpse of her beautiful body as some kind of retribution for cutting short the massage.

To what end? To remind him what he was missing? He *knew* what he was missing. Passionate romps in the bed of the sexiest woman he had ever met.

The longer they shared the same house, the more fascinating Tori became—to his abject misery. Infiltrating his dreams at night. Disrupting his focus on the job. How had she cast this lust-infused spell on him? Was it because he had pronounced her off-limits, categorizing her in his libido as forbidden fruit, so to speak? Did he want her because he was no good for her? Because his rational mind stated he couldn't have her?

With any other woman, he wouldn't lose hours of sleep and waste a client's time daydreaming. When it came to Tori, the ramifications of his choices escalated to an entirely different, for-the-rest-of-their-lives level. Emotional landmines dotted the landscape. One misstep could cost him everything.

A conversation on the TV whorled into his ear. Raising onto an arm, he peered at the actors. Their dialogue made no sense. A second ago, these guys had been dodging bullets. He'd lost track of the story.

He'd lost track of his life.

Shaking his head, he grabbed the remote as the cordless phone on a side table rang. He paused the movie. If he didn't answer the call, would Tori let the machine do its thing or interrupt her bath? A considerate housemate wouldn't force her to choose.

He scooped up the phone. The name radiating on the display pushed a lump of flour-and-glue paste down his throat.

"Jarrett residence," Brett spoke into the receiver, gaze darting to the suspended ceiling panels separating him from a naked, soaking, dripping-wet Tori.

A familiar baritone boomed in his ear. "Well, now, this isn't Ryan, and it doesn't sound like Cory. Tell me, who are you, and why are you answering my phone?"

Brett bolted upright. His movements jostled Rex. The beagle's muzzle rolled into the sofa arm. Rex grunted, and a back paw kicked the air.

"Mr. Jarrett! Uh, Marty. It's Brett Evans." A time machine whizzed him backward into his adolescence. His nerves jumped as if he were sixteen and had just been caught feeling up a girl on her father's porch. Except Brett had never felt up Tori—aside from that one night. And, to be precise, he'd felt her all over.

"Brett." A jovial note brightened Marty's tone. "Hello! How are you?" The man's voice quieted, and muffled conversation drifted over the line. "Linda, it's Brett Evans...Yes, Ry's friend...I don't know. I'll ask him." Marty's voice sounded in Brett's ear again. "Linda says hello. Are you visiting town, Brett? Is Tori handy?"

She certainly is, sir. In ways you'd never imagine.

Clearing his throat, Brett leaned his elbows on his knees. "I'm fine. Great, as a matter of fact. You?" His pulse decelerated to a steady pace. "Tori is upstairs. Uh, making coffee."

Rex's head lifted. The dog stared. "What?" Brett whispered to the hound. Were he a father, he'd prefer the fib about the coffee over the reality that he lusted after Marty Jarrett's daughter.

"I'm watching a movie on Ry's TV with your dog," Brett informed the man. "Although I guess Rex is Tori's dog now."

The beagle, seemingly appeased, burrowed his head into the couch corner. Gusty snores snorted from the dog's twitching nostrils.

Marty chuckled. "I imagine Tori is spoiling that merry hound. Ol' Rexster. We miss him. Linda and I are having the time of our lives. When did you get to town?"

"Two weeks ago tomorrow." Brett described his consulting gig. "I'm sorry I missed you and Linda. And Ryan."

"Yes, our son has suffered a bad spell. He managed to email the other day but said we shouldn't expect to hear again for several weeks. He needs time. We're trying to respect that."

"Understood. Tori explained about the divorce."

"A shame. It wasn't meant to be. I take it you're at Tori's for dinner?"

Brett hesitated. Tori received a call from her parents last Sunday, the day after he moved in. Hadn't she mentioned their arrangement?

"We ate earlier. She's cleaning up." Her body, if not the dishes. Definitely not his mind.

"I thought she was making coffee."

"Er, correct. She's cleaning and making coffee. I'm about to go help." While he was reinventing the situation, he didn't want her dad to consider him a slacker.

"Excellent. Please put her on. Linda wants to make tomorrow a road day, so we won't be calling at our usual time."

"Just a minute." Pressing Hold, Brett returned the handset to the charging unit and headed upstairs. Rex remained comatose on the couch.

Wind-slapped rain pelted the roof and windows as he entered the living room through the widened kitchen opening and made his way to the hall outside the bedrooms and bath. Tomorrow, he and John would tape and mud the drywall seams before affixing the arch. John planned to repeat the mudding/sanding process throughout the week while Tori and Brett were at work.

Brett had to admit, he'd enjoyed John and Lorelei's company today. And Daisy and her friend were cute beyond compare.

He rapped a knuckle on the bathroom door. "Tori? Your dad is on the phone. I put the downstairs handset on hold. Do you want the one from your room?"

"They're phoning *tonight*?" Splashing noises echoed from inside. "Is something wrong?"

"Not at all." Brett cringed. "Sorry. Your dad said tomorrow is a road day. He and your mom are having a blast on the hogs. I told him you were making coffee."

"Coffee?" Derision flooded her tone.

"Roll with it. He didn't seem to realize I'm living here. As far as he and your mom are concerned, I came for dinner. Now you're cleaning up and making coffee."

"Gotcha." More splashing noises carried through the door.

"Do you want the cordless?"

"Stay out of my bedroom, Brett. I'll talk to them in the kitchen. I need a glass of water anyway."

Her feet padded on the linoleum. In another moment, the door swept inward, and an exquisite sight filled Brett's vision. Tori wore her hair pinned up. Damp tendrils curled on her pink cheeks. Her honeyed-hazel eyes blinked wide and luminous as hot steam billowed into the hall. Water droplets beaded her bare shoulders, and a towel hugged her curves. She gripped the knotted terry cloth between her breasts. The thin fabric undulated to an inch above her knees.

Brett swallowed. "That must be some bath. Your skin is..." *Incredibly lick-able.* "...flushed."

She smoothed her hair. "It was very relaxing."

"Hey, who's Cory?"

She pulled back. "None of your business."

"It's just—um—your dad mentioned the name."

An angelic smile wreathed her face. Shouldering past him, she shut the door on the moist steam. Brett's gaze riveted to the wiggle of her towel-draped rear as she tracked water into the kitchen. Wet footprints dampened the hardwood in her wake. Helpful housemate that he was, he would wipe up the splotches.

Stepping into the bathroom, he reached for a hand towel. Hot steam blasted his face. He should switch on the fan. Excess humidity created mold. Before he had a chance to accomplish the task, his gaze swung to the extra-wide tub he and Ry had helped Tori's dad install as teenagers. Fragrant bubbles frothed the water, and a bright yellow rubber ducky bobbed along. The girly bathmat rippled askew on the floor.

Brett stooped to straighten the mat. A sheet of notepaper extended past the end of the fluff.

His fingers stilled. His brows shot up.

What do we have here?

8

CROUCHED BESIDE THE bathmat, Brett peered over his shoulder. The bathroom door remained open behind him and his ears pricked to the sound of Tori's voice murmuring into the landline a couple of walls and several yards away. He glimpsed her bright pink bathrobe on one of two brass door hooks. Why hadn't she donned the robe instead of wrapping her alluring hips and breasts in a skimpy towel? Didn't she realize he struggled with his attraction to her on an hourly basis? Didn't she *appreciate* his restraint?

Women—the most perplexing creatures on earth.

Tori Jarrett—their queen.

He returned his attention to the paper. Apparently, Queen Perplexing jotted renovation notes in the bathtub. Or something about that Cory character? She had seemed taken aback when Brett mentioned the name.

He couldn't take his gaze off the page. It practically pulsated with a siren's call to read it. Stifling a wave of guilt, he pinched a wad of damp mat between his fingers. His brows hoisted further. *Well, well.* Not only the sheet, but an entire spiral-bound notebook lay beneath the mat along with a Retro Vibe pen.

Teeth marks dented the pen cap, and Tori's rounded hand-writing looped in royal-blue ink across the page. Dampness curled the lower corner. Dried trickles of water smeared the title up top:

OPERATION UNDER THE COVERS

Capitalized and underlined, with fancy curlicues on either side.

Chuckling, Brett squinted. *Covers?* For the few pieces of living room furniture when they painted?

Careful not to disturb the notebook, he firmed his grip on the bathmat and examined the unobstructed page. A list appeared beneath the heading.

- *How to present the idea?*
- *Does it* need *presenting?*
- *Talk gets me nowhere. Just leap into it.*
- *Like a kiss. One kiss might work.*
- *Maybe it'll be awful.*
- *Crossing fingers it's HORRIBLE.*

Several empty lines followed. Air chuffed from his lungs. Who did she plan to kiss? Cory?

Jaw firming, he scanned a lone sentence:

- *When?*

Five large question marks occupied the middle of the page. The last two, outlined several times, gouged the paper.

Was she pissed off at Cory? Served him right, whoever he was.

His gaze drifted lower. *It's all about CHAD,* he read. *Seize the moment! Spontaneity is key.*

"Chad?" His voice emerged in a gruff whisper. He hadn't yet

climbed onboard with the concept of the Cory dude and now this chunk of chump change Chad was in the picture?

And who the hell *planned* spontaneity? Tori loved to-do lists. Was she to-doing Chad? Outlining the development of their relationship from kissing the guy—and hoping it was horrible for some insane reason—to crawling *under the covers* with Chump Change? Inviting Chad into her bed? A molten ball dropped in Brett's stomach as similarities to their night together smacked him between the eyes.

"Brett?"

Her voice! Winging from the kitchen, through the living room and into the hall. Clinching the back of his neck and squeezing his throat.

"My mom wants to know your mom's email address," she shouted.

He lowered the bathmat to how he'd found it.

"Brett?" Again with the yelling.

Thanking his lucky stars thick socks padded his feet, he quietly closed the bathroom and tiptoed into his bedroom via the hall door. Pasting on an innocent look, he opened the extra door into the kitchen. Hands stuffed in jeans pockets, he rambled in and glanced around, head bobbing. Chill as a freaking cucumber. "Yeah?"

She stood at the counter, upper arms clamping the towel against her sides. "Where were you?" she whispered, covering the phone's mouthpiece.

"Reading." Which was true. "In my room." Which was not.

"Where's Rex?"

"Downstairs."

Her head tilted. Her gaze traveled over his face for what felt like ten minutes but probably lasted three-quarters of a second. Whatever the time frame, for Brett the moment ticked into slow motion. A wisp of brown-sugar hair touched her cheek. Several more drying strands coiled on her neck. The effect was breathtakingly beautiful. His chest caved inward. His eyesight grew fuzzy. The edges of his peripheral vision dwindled into nothingness as his senses zeroed in on the lovely goddess holding the phone.

Tori. Tori-mine. She inspired poetic sensibilities in his prosaic soul. Outside the kitchen window, the downpour clobbered the earth, thunder rumbled, and distant lightening cracked, but inside Tori's house warm sunshine streamed and fragrant flowers blossomed.

What self-respecting guy thought that way?

The yellow towel hung loosely at her waist but shaped her hips and breasts.

Curves his hands had caressed.

Concealing secrets he had revealed.

And longed to see again.

Regardless of every logical reason he shouldn't.

"Brett?"

Her voice penetrated the long tunnel of his consciousness. "Uh?" Was he drooling? He closed his mouth.

She gestured at the phone. "Is your mom on Facebook?" Gooseflesh dotted her shoulders as the bathwater dissipated from her ivory skin. She poised a pen above a notepad.

"Hell if I know. Does the Retro Vibe have a page?"

"Facebook," she repeated. "A phone number? Email address? For your mom. Hello?"

"Oh. Ah. Right." A functioning part of his brain perused his rusty memory banks, called up the last two pieces of information, and instructed his lips and tongue to generate speech.

"Thanks." Arms squeezing the towel, she shooed him off.

Whistling to distract himself from the arousing effect of Tori wearing nothing but damp terry cloth, he tugged a kitchen rag off the oven door handle and wiped wet patches in the living room.

"Brett!" she called.

"Yeah?" He swabbed driblets in the hall. She needed to cover up before she froze to death.

"Don't go in the bathroom. My personal stuff is out."

"Righty-roo," he hollered, wondering how she might explain their loud exchange to her parents. He bit back a smile.

The hardwood dry, he reentered his bedroom and dug in the small closet for an old housecoat he recalled from her teen years. Polka dots and puppy dogs decorated the plush fabric. *Perfect.*

In the kitchen, he tossed the teen housecoat onto a nook seat. Tori, gazing out the rain-streaked window, chatted to her dad again, Brett surmised from the snippets of conversation about tractor museums. The towel sagged between her shoulder blades.

Lowering to his hands and knees, he swabbed the puddle of cool bathwater near her feet. She jumped.

"What are you doing?" she whispered, a line etching between her eyebrows.

"Being thorough."

"Make it quick."

"Right-o." The Bra Incident slammed to the forefront of his mind. *Had* she intentionally slipped him a peek the other night? Had she forsaken her thick robe for the thin towel for similar reasons? Specifically, utilizing *his* reactions as a testing ground for her plans for Chad?

He stifled a grunt. He wasn't a mannequin, impervious to her desirability. *He* wasn't a chump. He would clean the water mess as quickly—or as slowly—as he damn well pleased-o.

The rag bumped her foot, and her legs broke out in goose-bumps. Grinning, he crawled to the last footmark by the sink and mopped the spot. Knees cracking, he stood and slung the sodden cloth on the spout.

Tori hung up. "My parents say best of luck with your job." She held her arms in an X over the towel concealing her breasts. Her fingertips clenched her bare shoulders, the shiny nails digging tiny crescents into her skin.

"That was nice of them."

"And we might've found a music guy to round out that side of the store. He's the nephew of a friend of Mom's."

"Kudos." As long as he wasn't Chad.

"I'll contact him tomorrow. He sounds super promising."

"Fingers crossed." Brett looked around. No water glass in sight. He collected one from a cupboard and filled it at the tap. Stepping toward her, he extended the beverage.

"What's that for?" She eyed the tumbler like a hiker checking out a coiled snake.

"You said you were thirsty. I offered to bring the phone from your bedroom, but you said you needed water. So you came in here."

"Yes. Well." Her chin came up. "I can't drink it right now, can I?" She shivered in the damp towel. Lightning forked in the stormy sky, momentarily brightening the kitchen.

Brett glanced at the contents of the glass. "Promise you won't throw it at me?"

She snorted. "That depends. Why?"

"You're obviously cold. And, as previously determined, a mite parched. I have a solution." He set the glass beside the phone and retrieved the housecoat from the breakfast nook. "Stand still."

Her fingers shook. Her arms trembled. Her teeth chattered.

"Trust me, Tori. In another second, you'll be comfy-cozy." Moving behind her, he swooshed open the cushy fabric of the robe. Two puppy dogs winked at him. "I'll close my eyes." Averting his gaze and squeezing shut his lids, he pictured three dozen eager-eyed puppies and hundreds of multi-hued polka dots. "Okay. They're closed."

Considering her skill scooping her bra out the armhole of her top the other night, losing the towel and throwing on the teen robe should be a cinch for his good pal, Tori. Sister of his lifelong friend, Ryan. Daughter of standup folks, Marty and Linda. Under the mother-bear protection of her employee, Val. Interested in a guy named Chad.

And who knew what had happened with Cory?

A beat passed. Tori's breath hissed in as the towel landed on the floor.

A vanilla scent teased Brett's nostrils.

"You smell like sugar cookies," he murmured, clamping his lids tight. Tiny barbs of pain lanced his eye sockets.

"It's the bubble bath," she said as one of her arms meandered into a sleeve.

Puppies, Brett reminded himself. *Polka dots. Rex wolfing kibbles. Razor-sharp knives. Dismembered chickens.*

Nothing to this. He was on point.

Tori's second arm traveled into the other sleeve. Fabric swished. Elbows jostled, and the housecoat swept from his grasp.

Her feet padded away a step. "I'm done."

Brett opened his eyes. She'd pivoted to face him, and, damn, she looked fine sheathed in puppies and polka dots. The size of the housecoat wasn't an issue. The robe had hung a trifle large on her adolescent frame. Whereas now, it fit perfectly.

A sense of doom pervaded him. Tori had knotted the sash at her waist tighter than a twist-tie, and the fleece lapels cloaked her cleavage, but a pale blue polka dot perched directly atop the nipple of one breast and its round partner sat on the other.

The pink tint on his good pal's cheeks had deepened to an alluring rose. Her eyes glowed. *She* glowed. There was no other word to describe the luster of Tori Jarrett in full bloom.

Their gazes locked. Brett stood as if hypnotized. Without breaking eye contact, she grabbed the water glass and gulped several mouthfuls. Placed the glass on the counter and wiped her knuckles across a drop glistening on her lower lip.

"Cory is my ex," she blurted.

"Who?" Dense fuzz had set up camp behind Brett's forehead.

"Cory Price. My parents adored him. Everyone in my life thought he was awesome."

"Yes, yes." *That* Cory.

"We broke up last fall." An emotion—regret?—flickered in her eyes. "It was too bad."

Brett grasped her upper arm. "Was he an ass? Did he hurt you?"

"No." She pressed fingertips to her temple. "He was perfect. Everyone said *we* were perfect. But we were too perfect." She peered at him. "You know?"

Brett squinted. "Not a clue." He'd never experienced "too perfect" with a woman. Unless he counted Tori. And then he had run so fast and far—

Ah. He got it. "Too perfect" didn't work.

"We wanted the same things, but we shared too much in common. For some couples, that's boring."

"Cory said you were boring?" The concept didn't compute.

She shook her head. "We agreed—we were boring together. It was like we ticked off boxes for each other. We should have been a perfect match, but we didn't click. And in bed? It was a snooze-fest. Brett, I'm willing to wait for Mr. Right. I have faith he'll come along." She patted her chest. "I'm not in a rush. Not for a couple of years. Then, I admit, I might panic."

Information walloped Brett from a spinning wheel of directions. He opened his mouth, but no nuggets of wisdom ventured forth. He yearned to ask, *What about Chad?*

But he and Tori were *talking*. Discussing her relationship issues. The sort of thing friends talked about. This was good, right?

"Is there anyone currently?" For example, Chad?

She glanced away. "No."

"Anyone on the horizon?" Like, say, Chad?

"There'll be someone eventually." She picked a fingernail. "Maybe after you leave. I'm busy with the house and store right now. Mr. Right will show up."

"He'd be an idiot not to." Brett rubbed her arms. "You'll make a wonderful wife and mother."

She touched shaking fingers to her mouth. The barest shimmer of tears moistened her eyes.

"Tori, are you okay? Would you like more water?"

In the next instant, she grabbed his T-shirt. "Kiss me, Brett," she ordered, twisting the fabric in her fists.

"I—We—"

Her honeyed gaze pinned him. "Just once."

The words from her bathtub notes whipped through his mind. *One kiss might work.*

Did she want it to be horrible?

He blinked. Synapses fired. Was *he* Chad?

Why the hell would she call him Chad?

Gripping his shirt, she tugged him close, and their lips brushed. Their first kiss in four years.

Brett moaned. This wasn't what he wanted. It wasn't! But a sliver of light cracked open in his chest, releasing a buoyant, utterly foreign sensation, and he wasn't in charge of its escape. It had been lying in wait, like an alien creature living inside him without him consciously realizing it existed. Until—*holy crap*, here it was.

And he couldn't think. He could hardly breathe. Could only succumb to the power of the supernatural force shooting through his body. Connecting with Tori's lips and compelling him to deepen the kiss.

He cupped her face. The fingers of his right hand slipped to the rapid pulse beating in her neck. His tongue found hers. She released a tiny whimper, and they went deeper. Closer.

Brett felt like he was freefalling. Tori had pushed him out of an airplane without a parachute. In mere seconds, he would smack the ground. And then—game over. Nothing left but broken bones and mangled limbs. They would be done.

Heart hammering, he slid his hands off her face. Their mouths drifted apart. Entwining their fingers, he allowed their foreheads to touch.

"Let's do that again," she whispered.

"Tori," he murmured, "you're amazing. Every bit as beautiful"—*more* beautiful—"than I remembered."

Her breath hitched. "Thanks."

Stepping back, he glided a hand over her shoulder, the housecoat soft beneath his palm. "Tori, Tori, you're so tempting."

Her gaze implored, *Prove it, Evans. Kiss me.*

But his head was screwed on tight again. He wasn't Chad. Chad was some other guy. Chad was her future.

Whatever this was, sizzling between them, she deserved more.

"You're my Who," he uttered. He couldn't lose his Who. He *couldn't.*

Her voice squeaked. "You mean our old joke from the Christmas cartoon?"

The animated classic about the crusty geezer who tried to steal the holidays from the citizens of a tiny town. "Yes." Except, for Brett, the reference wasn't fun and games. He and Ryan and Tori had watched the film every school holiday as kids. The three of them plus Tori's parents huddled in front of the living room TV, sipping Mrs. Jarrett's marshmallow-topped hot chocolate and chowing down caramel popcorn.

Year after year, Tori's family had included Brett in their festive tradition. The kid from the neighborhood without a brother or sister. With a mom who worked double shifts Christmas Eve to ensure he woke up with abundant gifts under the tree.

How many times had he tickled Ryan's sister and teased the sweet little girl that she was his Tori Lou?

He busied his hands rearranging the lapels of her robe. The grownup Tori didn't say anything, just gazed up at him, gaze searching. Probing.

Finally, she stated, voice quiet but even, "Tori Lou was five or six, Brett. Do I look like a child to you?"

He inhaled raggedly. She didn't look at all like a child. That was the problem. He needed her safe in his heart. He couldn't risk losing her again.

"No," he croaked.

A saucy smile tilted her lips. "Do I kiss like a little girl?"

"I don't kiss little girls."

"You kissed Daisy goodbye today."

He screwed up his face. "On her cheek. Not her lips."

Humor danced in Tori's eyes. "We're in agreement then. On the lips is pervy. When kissing little girls. And let me be clear. By that, I mean children." She clutched his wrists and planted his palms on her hips. Crushed her full breasts against his chest. "Do I feel like a little girl?"

He heaved out a breath. "No. But you deserve better than a guy like me for a couple more weeks. If my staying here confuses things, I can find another hotel." The idea sounded less appealing than an ulcer chomping his stomach, but if she said the word he would leave tonight.

Her lashes fluttered. "Don't leave because of one tiny kiss," she said, voice husky. Aroused. A damned seductress, God help him. "You don't want me. I'll have to accept that." One shoulder lifted in an unconcerned shrug.

"I do want you." It was pointless to deny the evidence bulging in his jeans. "That doesn't change the facts. You're looking for Mr. Right."

"And I'll find him. Someday."

If her list about Chad—the name written in capitals on the notebook page now that he thought about it—was any indication, she wanted to find whoever or whatever CHAD represented sooner than she claimed.

"Tori, you need to think."

"I've been thinking since you walked through my front door."

"Then you need to think more." He scrubbed a hand across his mouth. "I won't be a party to hopping into bed with you again only to realize we've made another mistake."

She grinned. "Oh, it would be a party."

All right, he sounded like a by-the-book geek. But she wanted everything he wasn't.

"People learn from their mistakes," she said airily.

"You want me to be another mistake?"

"I'm saying it wouldn't be the worst thing."

"To be your mistake?"

"Your word. Not mine. Own your words, Brett. Think about it."

He drew in a breath. If he listened to her any longer, her logic might make sense. "Tori, you deserve your dream. I'm not your dream." He turned toward the stairs. "Goodnight."

Val's fork sank into her cheesecake. "Chocolate and peanut butter. My favorite. Great idea to come here after Meridy's and my shift, Tori." Val closed her eyes, smacking her lips. "Num-num."

Smiling at Val's antics, Tori picked at her own dessert in the outdoor cafe around the corner from the Retro Vibe. Two nights ago, she and Brett had shared a *yi-yi-yi* of a kiss before he'd abandoned her to descend into the basement and resume watching his movie, hogging even the soothing presence of her dog. Her white chocolate confection drizzled with raspberry sauce tasted like clumps of powdered milk.

"I'm concerned about leaving Nolan alone in the store," Meridy said, dabbing a napkin to her mouth. "It's his second day."

"Don't be." Tori shook her head. "He's volunteered at his uncle's jazz club for months. He shows initiative. I want to reward that." On the heels of Saturday night's drop-kick to the curb with Brett, she'd required a super-sized distraction. Texting Nolan and arranging an interview with the high school senior at the Retro Vibe for the next morning had provided solace for about two seconds. On the bright side, as soon as Tori and Nolan met, ideas for growing the music section of the store without sacrificing their faithful movie clientele dominated the conversation. Tori hired the student on the spot and supervised his first shift. If the summer went well, Nolan would remain on staff while attending Portland State's College of the Arts this fall. Snagging the millennial music major was a managerial miracle, if Meridy asked her.

"Running a cash register isn't rocket science. If Nolan can't handle a few customers while I'm on break, I need to know. He'll text if there's a rush."

Val waved her fork. "I do believe Meridy is more worried about you than the new guy. She's not crass like me, so she won't spit it out. What's up?"

A warm breeze sifted over the crowded patio, rustling Tori's hair. "Something wrong with treating my friends?"

Val's gaze narrowed. "It's Brett. Isn't it? Say I'm wrong."

How could she? "He kissed me Saturday night." Tori pierced a raspberry and swabbed the fruit in sauce. "Okay, I kissed him. He went along with it. For a bit." A blissful moment of paradise on earth. The man's lips were perfection, the light brushing of his fingers on her face decadently arousing. The lump in his jeans foreshadowing a multitude of pleasures to come. And come. And come again.

Except they hadn't progressed beyond the kissing.

Glancing at the surrounding patrons, she quieted her voice and described Brett interrupting her bathtub brainstorming session. Her impulsive decision to slap on a towel instead of her robe. Her nerves while they'd discussed Cory. The fortitude she'd rallied to step up her game and plant a wet one on his lips.

She left out the part about him calling her his Who. Who wanted to be a guy's Who? It was cute. She'd had it with cute.

"The kiss was incredible." Eons better than tangling tongues with Cory. Or any other man, if she was honest. Her best kiss in four years. She sighed. "Then he gave me that old song and dance about how we shouldn't have done it, he doesn't want to regret anything, blah, blah. He escaped downstairs, and I collapsed on my bed, feeling like a major fool."

"Did you follow him?" Meridy sipped her latte, gaze studious.

"Keep up, Mer. I hid in my room." After rescuing her notebook from the bathroom.

"Yeah, yeah." Val's fork clinked on her plate. "Went to your room. Felt like a fool. For how long? Please, sweetie, tell us you got your act together and skipped like the plucky duck you are downstairs." Setting aside her dessert, Val stared down Tori.

Dots of heat seared her cheeks. "That didn't happen."

Meridy gaped. "You're pressed against him, kissing, touching. He basically says you're sex on a stick but he cares too much to sleep with you, and you *don't* follow him?"

Val twirled a finger. "What you should have done was lose the towel and hop him in the basement."

"I couldn't," Tori half-whispered. "Rex was down there, and he's scared of storms. Either of you done it with a dog watching?"

Val scratched an eyebrow. "Actually, yes. It's not like pets take sex ed in school. They don't know what's going on. That's Wade's philosophy."

Meridy ran a thumb below her lower lip. "I suppose Rex might have sniffed them," she murmured to their friend.

"True," Val conceded. "Okay, the first time with a dog or cat around feels *meh*, but with the proper incentive—"

"Like a treat," Meridy broke in, gazing at Tori. "Rex would have settled quite happily in your room with a soup bone. No stuffing him in a doghouse during a thunderstorm involved."

Did these two not understand beagles? "He would have howled at the top of the stairs."

Val snickered. "Five bucks says Brett would have howled."

Tori plunged her fork into her dessert—and left it there. "You troublemakers have an answer for everything. Wanting to seduce Brett is one thing. Accomplishing it is hard."

Val winked. "It's supposed to be hard when you're doing it, girlfriend."

Tori smiled despite herself. "The man was everything I wanted for years. Did his assignment at Sugartree have to run a solid month?" Lordy-*Lou*!

"That must be some software," Meridy said, brows arched.

"She's the software. He's the hardware." This from Val.

"I can't get him off my mind. But if he's not into it, I...I..." Would forever wonder if another man could match the spark and sizzle and snappity-snap she and Brett shared. "I can't wind up with another Cory. I want the magic I feel with B. I just want it with someone else, and B is in the way. Does that make sense?"

"Totally," Val replied. "He's your gateway drug to a hot love life."

"Yes!" Tori flung out her arms. "I can't shake the feeling that there might be hope for me and CHAD. *After* I'm finished with Brett. What am I supposed to do? Why is he so stubborn? Why fight what we both obviously feel?"

Meridy propped an elbow on the table. "Because"—she pointed at Tori—"unlike you, my self-aware friend, he doesn't realize he's stuck in the past. He doesn't understand surrendering to the sizzle is the only way either of you can move forward. Tori, don't give up when you're so close. Brett needs this roll in the hay as much as you do. He's just too dense to add two plus two." She propped her chin on her palm. "Yet," she ended, eyebrows waggling.

"Hell, yeah!" Val yanked the fork out of Tori's dessert and pressed the utensil into her hand. "Now, eat," she admonished, curling Tori's fingers around the handle. "You need nourishment for the long nights ahead."

ori's Planner ~ Thought for the Day
    Sometimes you whine, sometimes you swoon

"HEY, JOHN." BRETT greeted the big man as the polythene curtains parted and John entered the kitchen, drywall dust from the living room coating his jeans and sweaty T-shirt. "How's the mudding coming along?"

"On schedule. A couple more rounds and the walls will be ready to prime."

Setting his laptop case on the nook table, Brett gestured toward the new arch. "It's a shame about Mrs. Jarrett's roosters." Installing the curved opening yesterday had necessitated removing a patch of Linda's Americana wallpaper. Some sort of 1960s wallboard peeked from the stripped area, and old spackle smoothed triple grooves at the seams.

"I dunno," John said with a chuckle. "I tore dinosaurs in party hats off my bedroom walls as a kid. Their eyes gave me the creeps." Stepping to the sink, he washed his hands. "Lorelei says

Tori is hanging paintable wallpaper in here to hide damaged spots until she renovates this space."

Brett nodded. At this point, John would know more than he did about Tori's plans for the kitchen. In the forty-eight hours since she'd traipsed out of the bathroom, water droplets beading her naked shoulders, he'd steered clear of the sexy nymph. What other choice did he have? A sour tang tinged his stomach. In a little over two weeks, he returned to Sacramento. They needed to resolve their issues STAT.

Apparently, she thought hopping into bed was the answer. *Uh, say what?* He'd wanted to earn his way back into her life, not damage their relationship beyond repair.

Rex howled on the porch. John jerked his chin toward the locked doggy door. "I packed up the stilts and mud. Rex is safe to come in."

Brett unlatched the panel, and Rex barreled inside, speckled forelegs pressed to the linoleum and butt and tail wriggling. Brett scratched the dog's ears. Clumps of grass and dirt flew off Rex's paws as the dog bounced out of reach and romped to his food bowl. Rex stared at Brett and whined.

John dried his hands, grinning. "Don't let that walking stomach fool you. Tori fed him before her shift."

Brett chided the dog, "Trying to pull a fast one on me, huh?" He pulled open the fridge door. "Have time for a beer?"

"Not today." John ambled to the porch door. "Lorelei is taking her mom to a movie. Daisy and I are playing dolls. Maybe tomorrow."

"Looking forward to it." A companionable chat with a happily married man like John Radford might provide some insight into the workings of the female mind. Brett was a ship sinking beneath the weight of a giant iceberg.

Alone with Rex, he sat on a nook seat and unlaced his wingtips. The dog raced in circles around the kitchen, lunging forward then bounding away.

"Yes, I got the memo." Brett grinned. "You want your walk. I need to change first." Pulling off his shoes, he glanced around. "Where's your leash?"

Rex skidded to a stop, floppy ears perking.

Brett checked the counters and usual drawers to no avail. He jogged downstairs, the dog a cheerful companion. Nothing there either.

They returned to the main floor. The beagle shadowed Brett as he searched his bedroom, the bathroom, the plastic-draped furniture in the living room, the front entryway. The chalky scent of freshly applied drywall compound saturated the air.

"What the—?" He glanced at the dog. "Where's your leash, boy?"

Rex pawed Tori's bedroom door.

"No way." Brett held up his hands. "She'd skewer my head."

Rex whimpered, snout lowering to hardwood.

"Dog, you're killing me." Hours of beagle-moping would now ensue. "Just a sec. I have an idea." He slipped his phone out of a pocket and texted John. *Looking for dog leash. You seen it?*

Two seconds passed. His phone dinged.

John: Check the bedroom. We were moving boxes from the attic before Tori left. Think I spotted leash on desk.

Brett's forehead furrowed. *In her bedroom?* he typed.

John: She misplaced her phone. Was running around. Pretty sure I saw leash.

Brett: I can't go in her room.

John: LOL. She got girl cooties?

Brett blinked. Another incoming message dinged.

John: What are you afraid of?

So many things inappropriate to discuss with the guy via text. Brett waited a moment before keying in, *Found leash. By front door.*

John: ??? That's the last place I mudded. Didn't see leash.

Brett: Hah. Get your eyes examined. Walking dog now.

Pocketing the phone, he looked at Rex. "I just lied for you."

"Roohhh." Saggy lips drooping, Rex scratched the bedroom door.

"Give me a break." Rex and Radford were in cahoots. "All right." Brett pointed at the dog. "This is on you."

Opening the door, he stepped inside the senior Jarretts' bedroom. Tori's bedroom. He held his breath. The space felt almost sacrosanct, a symbol of a successful marriage. A bond that strengthened with the passing years.

For not the first time since coming to Portland, he mulled over what it must be like growing up secure in your parents' love. Not wondering if a different woman might appear on your father's arm any given month—that was, if he managed to squeeze in a visitation. Not speculating how long your mom would remain alone, rarely dating. Sacrificing her happiness for yours every damn day.

A weight pressed on his chest. Hands on hips, he ignored the heaviness as best he could. A dark wood bedroom set dominated the cozy space. The boxes John had mentioned stood beside Tori's old kiddy desk featuring glossy white paint and drawers the color of spring grass. The top drawer hung partly open, as if she'd hurriedly located her phone and raced to work without a backward glance.

The blue handle of Rex's retractable leash lay on the floor. The cord stretched up to the drawer. The clip must have snagged on something inside.

Brett took a step toward the desk. Beagle nails clickety-clacked.

"Roo-oo-oohhhf!" Rex soared onto the bed like a superhero without a cape and rolled around on his back.

Not on the carefully folded dog blanket at the foot of the feminine bedcover.

Not on the second blanket forming a messy doggy bed a few inches below the nearest pillow.

But on the only unprotected portion of bedspread, directly beneath the second pillow.

"Hey! Get down."

Brett was fast, but Rex was faster. Well into a festive beagle breakdancing spree. Front paws flapping, rear legs poking up, happily groaning, snout burrowing, entire body wriggling. Shedding more tiny hairs than seventeen Persian cats—in a quarter as many seconds.

Brett grabbed Rex's collar.

"Roohf!" The hound wrestled free and let loose a full-body shake, ears helicopter-whirling. Hair scattered on the bed and sprinkled Brett's business clothes.

"Damn it, Rex!" He held an arm against the beagle's squirming body in a futile effort to lessen the destruction of Tori's cover.

Rex clamped his jaws around a mangled stuffed fox missing an ear. Hopping to the floor, Rex held the toy between his paws and gnawed its stomach.

A headache thumping at Brett's temples, he hauled the dog blankets off the bed. In minutes, his evening chores had expanded from walking the dog and sweeping the animal's tracking of dirt and grass into the kitchen to include laundering Tori's bedspread plus his favorite shirt and trousers while finding time to scarf down a sandwich before she returned from the store and he incurred her rightful wrath.

He yanked a corner of the bedspread covered in dog hair. It and one pillow landed on the floor.

Along with a floral-patterned notebook.

Brett stared, heart pounding. The notebook from Tori's Saturday night bath?

He glanced at Rex. The dog chewed the fox. Another second passed. Brett shouldn't—he really shouldn't—invade Tori's privacy. Wasn't it bad enough he'd peeked at her Under the Covers list?

He raked stiff fingers through his hair. Yes, it was bad. Inexcusable. The sort of behavior a ten-year-old might engage in, not a grown-ass software engineer.

Unfortunately, curiosity—plus the need to discover what made Tori tick, not to mention how the contents of the notebook might help him navigate the bog of their relationship—propelled him to grasp the spiral-bound pages before Rex noticed, of all things.

Straightening, he glanced at the dog again. Then the cover of the notebook.

A large white shipping label obscured the center portions of several lines of writing. The sticker proclaimed "GOB" in large hand-drawn letters.

"Gob?" he muttered, upper lip curling. What about Chad?

Flipping pages, he coasted past renovation notes and a line or two about sorority sisters and genderless roommates. *Him?*

A ball of anxiety burning beneath his solar plexus, he forced himself not to backtrack. He shouldn't snoop too much. He needed to invade her privacy…just a little. Specifically, had she written about their kiss or her future plans concerning Brett or the Chad guy?

Based on her reaction the other night, she hadn't appreciated

Brett saying she was his Who. His sugary sweetness. His damn light. In fact, she'd appeared to take the pronouncement as an opportunity to prove him wrong. Planting his hands on her hips, pressing her soft breasts against his chest, giving him a rock-hard—

He cut short the thought before his body's natural response kicked in.

His thumb rested on the curled bottom of the Under the Covers page. Slowly, he slid his palm beneath the sheet and—casually, nonchalantly, as if the following words wouldn't affect him one way or the other—turned the page.

It was blank.

She hadn't written in the notebook since their kiss.

His shoulders sagged. From relief—or disappointment? How would he know? As Tori had accused the day she'd drenched his clothes in water, his emotional take on such matters sucked.

One thing was clear. Their kiss hadn't merited an entry.

An odd sensation shifted in his stomach. He flipped back the page preceding Under the Covers.

Also blank.

Throat squeezing, he turned back another page.

Pay dirt. The breath swooshed from his lungs.

Four large block letters sat at the top.

CHAD

In shimmering gold ink.

Beneath each letter, a squiggly arrow in hues of pink and minty green and silver pointed to a corresponding word:

- Caring
- Hard-Working
- Attractive
- Dad-Material

"Hah!" His suspicions were correct. CHAD wasn't a name. It was an acronym. A checklist for the qualities Tori longed for in a husband.

Rubbing his chin, he contemplated the list. A clever person might present the case that he matched two out of four characteristics. Fifty percent. Not too shabby, if he said so himself.

He was *Hard-working*. Who could dispute that? He worked himself ragged, although he was beginning to suspect his devotion to DataPrimer was more of a bandage covering whatever in life was passing him by than anything else.

But back to the list.

As each of his former friends-with-benefits had enthused, he was *Attractive*. Hey, they hadn't been dumb women. If one had drooled a time or two, common sense dictated his looks were presentable.

And you know what? He peered over his shoulder at Rex, who munched a hind leg on the fox. He returned his attention to the list. He *Cared*. Maybe not how Tori wanted or needed or deserved, but still. He cared. About her.

In a way that suddenly made his insides resemble a squishy marshmallow. One a careless camper might split in half while spearing on a pointed stick for roasting over a raging campfire spitting sparks and billowing smoke. If the marshmallow didn't toast to the camper's liking—if her stick drooped into the flames and the treat charred to a crisp—it wasn't a stretch to imagine her stomping the gooey remains into the earth beneath a clunky combat boot before choosing another for her stick.

Because God knew she had her pick of every freaking marshmallow in the bag.

Man, that would feel like utter crap.

Shaking off the disturbing images, he grumbled, "Forget the first three traits"—Caring, Hard-working, Attractive—"you miserably fail at number four." *Dad-material*. The quality Tori most desired. A man who shared her core values.

Chest aching, he allowed his gaze to drift down the page. Tori's handwriting declared:

I want to find CHAD. But Brett is—ugh!—in my face. Why can't I shake him off? Why does thinking about That Night—the part before he acted like a dick, at any rate—make my toes curl and my girl parts wet?

Wet?

I need to persevere. Get through, get around, get over Brett. For CHAD!

"Get over Brett," he mumbled. "Gob." Had she needed to use a disagreeable acronym? Like he was mucous in her mouth?

He considered her his light...and she considered him gelatinous glob.

He focused on a doodle of silver bubbles brimming a pink champagne glass. To the right of the glass, in shimmering gold, Tori had written:

For CHAD!!!

Laid out plain as day, a toast to her future. Without him.

His shoulders slumped. Was this how Tori had felt the night of Ryan's wedding? This past weekend, following their kiss, when he'd lectured her to think and she'd thrown his words in his face, had she felt achy and tender and anguished?

Rex's wet nose prodded his pants leg. The dog gazed up with imploring brown eyes.

"Your walk. Sorry, boy. I got distracted." Brett repositioned the pillow—miraculously free of dog hair—atop the sheets and stuffed the notebook beneath it. "Does she keep this here?"

The dog offered a vacant stare.

"Right. You don't actually speak."

"Roohf."

"Yes, I know sometimes you speak when I say speak—"

"Roohf!"

"Forget it." Brett needed the leash.

Stooping, he peered into the open desk drawer teeming with multi-colored pens, fancy paperclips, and rolls of patterned tape. The clip end of the leash hooked onto the large coil binding of a two-inch-thick notebook. He scraped open the drawer and, fingers buried in Tori's stuff, worked to free the leash.

Rex jumped up, clawing his leg.

"Ouch! Crap, dog!" *Shoot. Don't crap in the house, dog. Please don't crap on command.*

Brett unhooked the leash. The big notebook scooted to the right, exposing a squiggly heart in faded pink marker on the bottom of the drawer:

Tori + Brett 4-Ever

The year jotted beside the heart indicated she'd created the doodle at around thirteen.

Brett released a low groan. He was an asshole. The evidence stared him in the face. Tori had suffered his teasing as a kid and, apparently, carried a torch for him as a young teen. At twenty-two, she conspired to lose her virginity—to him.

His thoughts beelined to their spirited debates when he'd first arrived in Portland. How had she cushioned her reasoning about the sequence of events the night of Ryan's wedding?

The words bubbled up. "Oh, right." She'd wanted to pop her cherry, *with a guy I thought I could trust.*

She had trusted him, and he'd let her down, escaping to Sacramento at the first opportunity. She hadn't been clear about the state of her...virtue...but he had fled.

He squinted at the notebook. Now she needed another sexual romp as part of an elaborate effort to put their past behind her?

So she could move forward and ultimately fall in love with CHAD?

Did he have that right?

Tori deserved happiness. Was it Brett's fault she hadn't found it?

He grunted. He didn't like this. Any of it!

Mind a blur, he clipped the leash onto Rex's collar and shut the drawer. Tori knew what she wanted and had executed a plan to achieve her vision. He was nothing more than a pawn on the chessboard of her life. Yet he couldn't bring himself to cast any blame her way. His behavior—during the past several years and over these last two weeks—had led them here.

Chest a gaping wound, he looked at Rex. Breathed in. And out. Pain wracked his ribs.

"Houston, we have a mother of a problem."

The kitchen was a sauna. So *not* Portland, even for mid-June. But Tori had long ago learned that a hefty dose of conviction paired with a fervent dollop of faith could power her through darn near any situation. Including baking cookies for Daisy's class party while another heat wave smothered the city and Brett "You're my Who" Evans secreted himself away at Sugartree.

Baking calmed her. She sorely craved the tranquility after two more days of sharing her house with that man. Honestly, if she married a guy who called her his Who, she would consider the sentiment utterly romantic. In Brett's case, however, as far as she could tell, the label provided a handy barricade against their mutual desires. Because the attraction was mutual. He couldn't deny he wanted her, which marked a progression of sorts, but a woman could only handle so much of a guy standing on principle regarding ancient history. And lately, when Brett was home, he tiptoed around the place with an aggrieved expression on his too-handsome face, his gaze now and then casting her direction as if he feared she might launch a vampire-leap from on high and sink her teeth into his neck. Drain his hottie body bloodless.

Not that he wouldn't deserve it. What was up with the eggshell routine? He'd walked away from her Saturday night. That didn't mean they couldn't exchange a few pleasantries during his remaining stay.

Perspiration trickling between her shoulder blades, she tapped a playlist on her phone and tied an apron over her bikini. As an up-tempo favorite trilled from the speaker, she reminded herself Brett's issues weren't her responsibility. His struggle against 'surrendering to the sizzle,' as Meridy had described it, wouldn't affect full-steam-ahead, focused-on-the-future Tori Jarrett. She would Keep Calm and Bake On. She was gonna bake Brett off.

The stand mixer hummed and whirled as she measured ingredients into the bowl and scraped her spatula along the glass. Within moments, her blood pressure stabilized.

The porch door opened.

"Hey, Tori."

Her blood pressure spiked.

Glancing over her shoulder, she affected a cheerful chirp. "Brett. You're home early." He carried two pizza boxes. For dinner? Her heartstrings pinged.

She firmed her chin. Hold up. He couldn't ignore her for days then buy her off with the surprise of delicious-smelling takeout. Not immediately, at any rate.

Gaze wide, he eyed her bikini-clad rear. "Why the bathing suit?"

Brushing clammy hair off her forehead, she faced him. The flip flops on her bare feet squeaked as she presented her butt to the stand mixer. Her apron concealed her curves from upper chest to mid-thigh—about as sexy as sporting a spaghetti-strapped gunnysack and gumboots halfway up her shins.

And you know what? She couldn't care less.

"Don't freak out, Evans," she said with a jaunty hike of her eyebrows. "I didn't doll up for your benefit." This time. A sliver of guilt inched beneath her skin. "Heating the oven made me hot." She fanned a hand in front of her face. The Sugartree complex and Brett's rental car both featured air conditioning. He looked wonderfully cool in a button-down shirt rolled up at the sleeves, exposing sculpted, lightly tanned forearms. No matter. The interior of her house would wilt him soon enough.

He set the pizza boxes on the counter. "What are you baking?" he asked, voice wary.

"Chocolate chip cookies for Daisy's class party tomorrow." Tori explained John's failed attempts to duplicate his deceased mother's recipe and Lorelei's plan to help her husband save face.

A small smile tilted Brett's lips. "They're good together, aren't they? Lorelei and John."

"Yes, they are."

He'd pointed this out, why? To remind her *they* were not?

The Radfords put each other first in small, everyday ways, a caress of the hand here and a tender glance there conveying an emotional and physical connection. Everything Tori wanted in a future relationship. Despite her failed attempts at piquing Brett's interest, she wished the same for him. The idea of the boy she'd known spending his life alone, convincing himself he was better off not having children or a woman to love or even enjoying the simple pleasure of belonging to a community, broke her heart.

Sighing, she sprinkled salt into the spinning cookie mixture before ejecting the beaters and setting the mixer aside. She moved the bowl onto the nook table and dumped in half a package of chocolate chips and stirred them into the batter with a wooden spoon.

Brett stepped to the table. His enticing sandalwood scent intermingled with the yummy-smelling dough as he scooped a chocolate-chip-dotted dollop out of the bowl. He assessed her with a sideways glance. What was he waiting for?

"Thanks for buying pizza," she said carefully. "I'm not eating until the cookies are in the oven. You go ahead. Need a plate?"

"Where's Rex?" Brett swirled his tongue around the clump of dough on his right index finger. The finger that, one fateful night, had glided leisurely down her breast and over her nipple, bringing it to a stiff—

Swallowing, she gestured her mixing spoon toward the basement. "Mick walked the dog for an hour. He took along a water dispenser, but the poor baby was beat when they got back."

"Poor baby?"

"Rex." Who else? "He's having a siesta." On the couch the dog often lounged upon with Brett. "The basement is the coolest spot in the house today."

"Mick walked him?" Brett quizzed in the manner of a newbie detective checking holes in a suspect's story.

Nodding, Tori folded chocolate chips into the dough. "Isn't that nice? He offered to walk Rex the days we're painting. Today was a test-walk."

Brett's gaze meandered around the hot kitchen before settling on her apron. "You weren't wearing your bikini when he picked up the dog? Or dropped him off?"

Her moist cheeks blazed. "Of course not." *Sheesh*. She wasn't a twenty-first-century Mrs. Robinson!

Brett inhaled. "*Take Whisks*," he murmured, quoting the saying on her apron. His gaze rose, meeting hers.

Tori's neck hairs, even the sweaty ones, stood on end. She emptied the second portion of chocolate chips into the bowl.

"Tori, we need to talk."

Lordy-Lou, he sounded ominous. "Is it your mom?" Her heart hammered her ribs.

"No."

"Your dad?"

"No." A dazed, confused, and trifle-constipated expression pinched his features.

"Then who?" The suspense jacked her pulse. She stood remarkably motionless, dough-coated spoon in hand as she allowed Brett the eternity evidently required to disseminate the unspoken words vibrating in every corner of her kitchen. The next song on her phone's playlist declared the singer and her ex were never ever getting back together.

He crossed his arms. "I'm not sure how to say this." He paused. "It's Chad."

"Okay." First she'd heard of the guy. "A friend?" At Sugartree?

"Not *Chad* as in the name Chad." Brett frowned. "C-H-A-D," he spelled. "CHAD. Your CHAD."

"My"—Tori hiccupped—"CHAD?" Segments of information assembled in her brain like an image depixelating on a screen. *Lordy-Yi!* "You read my notebook?" White-knuckling the spoon, she managed not to shriek.

"Just one page. Saturday night, while you were on the phone." He winced. "I spotted it in the bathroom by accident. *By accident,*" he emphasized.

How could he have committed this atrocity by accident? "I said my private stuff was out. I said, 'Don't go in.'"

"You did," he agreed, a finger bouncing up. "After I went in. But it's all right. We can fix this. I only meant to turn on the fan. You know, to prevent mold. Instead I bent to fix the bathmat. That's when I noticed a page sticking out of the bottom, and I…" His Adam's apple bobbed. "…read it."

He might as well have squirted pepper spray into her eyes, because they burned like miniature suns. He had read her embarrassing Operation Under the Covers brainstorming?

She held her breath until the tension bulged in her throat. "*Brett!*"

He lifted a hand. "I read a bit more Monday when you were at work. The page explaining what the letters in CHAD mean. That time was in your bedroom."

Her jaw hit the floor. "You snooped? In my room?" As if they were kids. *Everything* related back to their childhoods. She was over it!

"I only wanted to walk Rex. To be nice, like Mick," he added, as if the comparison held merit. "John suggested I check your desk for the leash. Rex jumped on the mattress and made such a mess, I can't tell you. Dog hair everywhere. I figured you'd have my head if you saw that," he continued with the reasonableness of the incurably insane, "so I decided to do laundry." His hands spread open. "Don't ask me where the notebook was in the bed. I dragged off the covers, and it fell on the floor. I had a gander—"

A gander?

"—at a couple of pages before stuffing it under your pillow. This is horrible and immature, and I deserve to be strung up. I've been going nuts wondering why you haven't said anything."

Invisible heat blisters popped open on her face. She gritted her teeth. "I've. Been. Busy."

He emitted a scratchy laugh. "I can't believe I put everything back right."

"You read it," she seethed. Her hopes and dreams and plots and schemes. Was that why she'd found the notebook wedged between the bed frame and wall when she'd returned from work Monday night? Had the volume slipped after Brett stuffed it beneath her pillow? She hadn't purposely stored it there. John had arrived that morning to mud, interrupting her perusal of the entries. She'd buried the notebook in her sheets before they lugged clothing boxes from the attic.

Dammit. Between hiring and training Nolan, fretting about the advice her friends had dispensed over cheesecake, and coordinating the house renovations, Brett's maneuverings had escaped her notice. Now his peculiar behavior over these last few days made sense.

Tone lethal, she held the wooden spoon inches from his nose. "What else did you read?"

His hands came up. The guilty, under arrest. "Not all of it. Enough to understand what you want. Want you need."

"Oh, yeah?" This should be good. "And what might that be?" She shook the spoon. A wad of dough flopped onto the floor.

A ruddy hue washed his cheekbones. "To bury the hatchet. In your way. So you can go on with your life. Man, it's warm in here." He tugged his shirt collar.

Bury the hatchet? He didn't understand her. Not one little bit.

"I wanted to find closure with you, Brett." A sob slipped from her mouth. "I wanted you to see me as a woman." She splayed a palm on her upper chest. "Not as Ryan's little sister. Not as a pal." She breathed in on a ragged gasp.

He rested a hand on her shoulder. "Tori, what I read or didn't read isn't the point. I've realized"—his voice lowered—"I can give you what you need." His eyes twinkled. "You know, under the covers."

She jerked away. "You can, huh?" She waggled her spoon. "*Now*, after snooping in my stuff not once but twice, *now* you're offering to *sleep* with me?" Was the man seriously presenting her with the gift of his hotness?

A pained look crinkled his eyes. "That's what you want. From the few pages I read. Right?"

"Not anymore. Not like this! Like you're doing me a favor." She plunged the spoon into the cookie mixture and flourished her fingers over her apron-and-bikini-clad body. "You'd be lucky to get up in this, Evans."

Befuddlement twerked on his face. "But you said I did do you a favor four years ago. That's why you kept your virginity a secret. You trusted me to help you out."

"And look where that got us." Him running to California. Her brokenhearted. "I wanted this time to be spontaneous."

He shook his head. "Except it's not. You've been orchestrating it."

The truth of his words pierced her clean through. She couldn't look at him.

Snatching a paper towel, she swiped cookie dough off the floor before Rex woke from his post-walk stupor and emerged from the basement to gobble chocolate chips.

As she strode to the below-sink cupboard and chucked the waste in the trash, Brett said, "For me, four years ago was spontaneous. But you planned it."

One eyelid twitching, she dusted her hands on her apron. *Smackety-smack.* Cleaning up her mess. "Not every minute. Or hour. Or even that day." She huffed. "Did I want you to take my virginity? Yes. Did I pull your strings like some puppet master? No. There was something between us the week before the wedding. There was a two-way attraction that night. Not just me, and not just you, Brett. It was us both."

She pinched her thumbs to her forefingers. Nails stung flesh. "There's an energy sparking between us now." She wished to hell it were otherwise. "But I'm over it. I'm sick of rehashing four years ago. I don't care what you read about CHAD. I am done." Because suddenly she got it. Unless she put a stop to the madness, she and Brett were doomed to repeat their mistakes over and over. Two hapless souls caught in a *Groundhog Day* time-loop.

Except they wouldn't wise up and miraculously solve their problems. No matter how many times Tori pretended not to agonize over her inability to find Mr. Right and Brett attempted to soften the blow that it wasn't him, the month ended with him returning to Sacramento and her soldiering on, seeking a happiness which, for all she knew, would forever remain beyond her grasp.

And she would have to live with that.

"Tori, calm down." Roughness edged his deep voice. "Maybe I shouldn't have said anything about CHAD or the notebook, but it seemed only right."

She swept her hands over her sticky face, scraping back her hair. "No, I'm glad you told me. I'm not proud of what I've done. But, I have to say, you coming clean just now has shown me the light." She pointed at herself then him. "My feelings aren't your responsibility." The mirror opposite of what she'd been thinking in the seconds before he'd walked in the door. She needed to work through her crap. And she would. On her own. "So, thank you, Brett, for helping me confront my crazy."

Gaze clouding, he stepped forward. "We're over?"

"'We' were never real. It was just my—" Stupid, stupid heart. "I can handle being friends." She presented a watery smile. "Without benefits. No more games. We're childhood buddies who made a colossal mistake one night. Nothing more or less." She hauled in a long breath. *Wow*. It felt good to say that. Brett didn't need her insecurities muddling his life when dozens of knots required unraveling on his end.

She understood. Finally, she got it.

What a relief.

10

BRETT STARED AT Tori standing by the nook table, hair mussed around her face and eyes red-rimmed with stress. Perspiration beaded in the hollow of her collarbone, and flour freckled her cheeks and bare shoulders. The ties of her bikini top disappeared into her apron, which had loosened as they'd squabbled. The fabric sagged, wrinkling *Take Whisks*.

He had never been so turned on.

What was wrong with him? The woman kissed him, and he walked away. She agreed to be his pal, and panic strapped tight bands around his chest.

"It's settled, then?" His abs clenched. "We're friends?" *Without* benefits. Buddies. Chums. *Chumps*.

"Yep." She blew a strand of hair off her lips. "I'm totally fine with it. No worries." She fist-bumped his arm. The imprint on his shirtsleeve clung to his hot skin.

He didn't believe her. "And…you're calm?"

She studied the ceiling. "I think so."

Then why did he feel like he might fall through a sheet of ice any second? "Be patient with me, Tori." He pressed his palms toward the floor. "I've spent the last couple of days coming to grips with what I thought you wanted. What I figured you were up to."

Her gaze slivered, and the crashing-through-ice sensation intensified. "Clarify 'up to.'" Her head tilted.

"You've been trying to get my attention." He paused. "In a romantic sense."

Red splashed her cheeks. "Don't you dare mock me, Brett."

"I'm not. I want to understand."

She gazed at him for a tension-filled moment. "All right," she said, moving to the bowl of cookie dough and stirring. "You said to think. Apparently, I listened. Weird, huh?"

It couldn't be that simple. Not with Tori Jarrett. "But you're turning on a dime here. That's not like you." He sliced both hands up and down, palms inward. "You establish goals and create strategies to achieve them."

"Well, I can't have everything I set my sights on, can I?" She directed a sardonic smile over her shoulder. "I learned that when Mom and I needed to revamp Jarrett's Video into the Retro Vibe. Businesses evolve with the times. The same philosophy applies to relationships." She shrugged. "The way I see it, I'm making a mature decision to stop acting like a high school cheerleader hoping to catch the eye of the hot new quarterback. I mean, what's the point? All he cares about are touchdowns and college scouts."

"Touchdowns and—?"

"His career." Tori leveled him a get-with-the-program look before stepping to a drawer for two teaspoons. "Take your pizza and go eat somewhere." She flicked a hand. "I'm fine."

He wasn't fine, and he seriously doubted she was.

"The pizza can wait. I'm staying put."

"Then make yourself useful. Find some cookie sheets. Check the oven drawer." Pivoting on her flip flops, she clasped the spoons and retrieved a box of aluminum foil from a lower cupboard. Her bikini bottoms slid up her rear as she bent over, exposing an inch of juicier-than-sliced-watermelon flesh.

Brett's lungs ceased functioning for a mind-bending moment. Heart thudding, he forced moisture down his throat.

Damn it, there *was* a program and he'd only now realized its existence. Why hadn't he seen this coming? Why had he discounted what suddenly seemed obvious and inevitable? If he and Tori were pals, a glimpse of her behind in a swimsuit wouldn't fog his brain worse than summer mornings along the California coastline. He might react with standard-issue male excitement but not this fiery hunger.

His need seared his skin as fiercely as it had the night of Ryan's wedding. The fissure which had made itself known beneath his ribs four days ago widened. The resounding crack boomed in his ears.

And just like that, he knew.

This was what he'd been wrestling with since spotting the notebook. Not the impossibility of polishing Tori's future until it glowed with certainty and promise, but what she and he required from each other in the here and now.

He couldn't deflect anymore, and he refused to allow her to mask her hurt beneath another show of bravado. Neither of them escaped unscathed in that scenario. Before he left Portland, he needed to feel he'd done everything within his power to help this amazing woman achieve closure on their battered past. Anything less seemed glaringly selfish.

"The cookie sheets?" she asked, glancing at him with the spoons and foil in hand.

"Still in the oven drawer." As pop music tinkled from the counter, he dipped a thumb into the bowl of cookie dough and smeared a dot on the tip of her nose.

Her eyebrows dipped. "What are you doing?"

"Being spontaneous." He scooped out a two-fingered clump.

She thumped the spoons and foil on the table. "Those are Daisy's cookies."

"Not until they're baked. The raw stuff is up for grabs." He dabbed chocolate chips and dough on her chin.

She gasped. "Brett Hennessy Evans!" She swiped the sticky mess off her face. Gooey bits flung from her fingertips, smacking his temple and rolling down his ear. Eyes rounding, she clapped a hand over her mouth. "That was an accident."

"A likely story." Brett bolted for the bowl.

Tori reached it first, pelting blotches onto his shirt.

Clasping her waist and spinning her around, Brett pinned her wrists at the curve of her spine. She squealed, her rear bumping his pants zipper. His shoe skidded on a slippery clump, and her knees collapsed. He broke the fall as they went down. She rolled over on top of his chest, giggling and breathless.

Their noses touched. Tori's messy hair veiled his face. Her apron twisted between their bodies, the neck loop completely undone and coiled on the floor. She curled her hands into small fists beneath her breasts, which swelled in her bikini top. Brett cupped her bottom. Velvety skin warmed his fingertips, and his erection ached.

"Brett," she murmured, voice husky. "We decided. We're pals."

"You decided," he responded gently, brushing hair off her face, "just as I figured out we weren't." He grazed a thumb along her jaw. "Tell me no, Tori. Or tell me yes. For old time's sake."

A breath wisped into her mouth. "Are you sure you want to do this?" she half-whispered. "Because I'll be okay. Will you?"

A hollow ball pitted in his stomach. "I don't know." Which terrified him. "I have no idea what I'm doing with my life. I thought I did but—" He broke off. His next words might sound ridiculous, but he needed to explain the Tori Effect. "Did you learn about the Berlin Wall in school?"

She nodded, the long strands of her hair tickling his ears.

"Our history teacher played clips of East Berlin before the Wall came down. She traveled there with her boyfriend when she was young. The Soviets erected the barricade around West Berlin, but if you were in a western sector, it felt like the Wall surrounded the East."

"The symbol of the Cold War." The corners of Tori's mouth tipped up. "I think we had the same teacher."

"Then you heard about the day they passed through Checkpoint Charlie," Brett continued through a tight throat. "She said it felt like they'd stepped back in time. It didn't help that it was an overcast Sunday and they were proud Americans." He smoothed away flour specks on Tori's cheeks, scant inches above his face. "They remembered bullet holes in the shells of buildings bombed in World War II and never repaired. Armed guards at dingy old subway stops where they couldn't get off. The massive war memorial in Treptower Park. The mood was overwhelmingly oppressive. When they crossed back into West Berlin, it felt like the sun came out again. The western sectors pulsed with life."

"Hmm." Tori's lips pursed, warmth flooding her expression. "In this analogy, am I West Berlin or East Berlin?"

"I'm East," Brett said. "You're West. Before I knocked on your door, I could see the wall in my own life. I had an inkling something incredible lay beyond the concrete. But I didn't realize how vibrant the world was on the other side." He gazed into her eyes. "Now I do, and I want a taste."

"That," she breathed, "is the loveliest thing you've ever said to me, you paint-by-numbers man."

"Will you let me in?" His chest throbbed.

Tori's lips swept his mouth. "There's no way I'm leaving you on the gloomy side of the wall."

This is happening. It's really happening.

Hands darting between her bed and dresser, Tori tidied her room while Brett coaxed her dog into the backyard. Any second now, the man who held the key to her future happiness would appear in her bedroom doorway and they would—*gulp*—get down and dirty. Frantic and fabulous. Underdressed and overwhelmed.

She was up for it. Yes, she was. She just needed to clear her head. Except she had no time to process whatever had sparked between them on her kitchen floor. Whenever she thought she'd figured out how to deal with Brett, he said or did something to spin her around. First, she was his pal. Then his Who. Now his West Berlin. If she were the sort to romanticize the symbolism of bashing down a decades-old, several-foot-high wall, the reference might go to her head. But she wasn't that girl.

Neither could she abandon her friend to a life of isolation, especially not at this surprising juncture. The realization that Brett had grown to perceive her as a portal to approaching the coming decades brimming with optimism instead of choking on a soggy sort of ennui touched her deeply. For once, they were on the same page.

She dug a box of condoms out of her nightstand, withdrew a packet, and tore open the foil.

What next? She glanced around. Wet wipes!

Snatching a moist towelette, she cleaned the dough and perspiration layering her upper chest and arms before kicking off her flip flops and stacking them atop her folded apron on a chair. She ran a brush through her sticky hair. Swiped another towelette over the bridge of her nose. Ate a chocolate chip nestled in her cleavage. Adjusted her bikini top. Smoothed the bottoms over her butt. Freaked out.

Where was he? What if he'd changed his mind? What if he showed up with TV-dad-in-lecture-mode lines creasing his mouth? She couldn't handle another rejection.

Footfalls sounded in the hall. Pulse going haywire, Tori fanned both hands in front of her face. Fainting was not an option.

"Tori?" Brett rounded the doorframe, face cleaned of dough and buttons half-undone, shirttails flapping. Hopping on one foot, he yanked off a shoe. Then the other. "I buried dog biscuits throughout the yard and locked the pet hatch. Rex is on a treasure hunt."

"Great idea." Tingles vibrated along Tori's skin as Brett threw off his shirt, unbuckled his belt, and chucked socks and shirt to the floor. Her fingers itched to trace the hard planes of his chiseled chest and abs. To run her palms along his sexy five o'clock shadow. To cup his face in her hands while they kissed. And never let go.

Urgency mounting, she stepped forward. He raised a hand.

"Stay there. I want to look at you." His hungry gaze consumed her face and breasts as he pushed his pants down his strong legs. Forest-green boxer-briefs outlined the thick ridge of his arousal. An instant later, he'd whisked away both garments, and his erection sprang into view.

Moisture gathered between Tori's legs. *"Brett."* Her nipples pointed in the bikini cups.

"I can't promise finesse this first time," he said, scooping her into his arms and caressing her upper back. "It's been too long. Four...suffocating...soul-sucking years."

The earthy choice of words rang absurdly romantic as his hands stroked behind her neck, beneath her hair. His fingers loosened the top string. The bikini cups sagged between their bodies, and her naked breasts pressed against his broad chest. He yanked open the back tie. The top fluttered to hardwood.

"Finesse is overrated." She wanted him hard and fast—before she burned up—and not from the stifling heat. Her need for this special man radiated from her molten core to the tips of her limbs.

"Woman, you light my world."

Her tummy swooped at his tender tone. *Not good.* She needed to protect herself from the rejection that might occur once they were done.

"Stop talking." She whipped off her bottoms. His hands grasped her rear, and he nestled her against his stiff length. They fell onto the bed, Tori beneath him, the sheets silky-smooth on her skin. His hands glided up her neck, and he cradled her head as his mouth came down to meet hers in a wet, hot, deep, passionate kiss. He tasted like cookie dough. Like sugar and chocolate and need and desire and *oh-my-yes-right-now-I-want-you-now*.

Tori moaned into his mouth. Not once did their lips and tongues break contact as he propped on his elbows and skated their bodies to the head of the bed. A pillow cushioned her neck, and her hair fanned out over the case. She inched one palm between their torsos, grazing a dusting of chest hair.

Brett's heartbeat thudded beneath her fingers. His head lifted, and his gaze fixed on her face, the hint of a smile curving his lips.

Something inside her turned topsy-turvy, delicate as crocuses blooming on a balmy spring morning following a gray-for-days rain.

"What?" she whispered.

His smile widened. "You're beautiful."

She cocked her eyebrows. "And persistent."

"Yes. Thank God." He kissed her again, gently. With arousing affection. His lips plucked hers in light caresses.

Brett. Her friend...and lover. *Again*. After an eternity without him.

How had she managed to continue existing?

His hand covered a breast, fingers teasing the nipple into a peak of sensation. Their kisses deepened. Corkscrews of longing tumbled inside her as she lowered her hand to his hard shaft, squeezed and stroked. A groan issued from his mouth.

"Protection," he said roughly.

"On the nightstand. But we don't strictly need it. Depending."

Sexual interest glowed in his eyes. "On what?"

"I'm on the pill...but there hasn't been anyone in months." A lot of months. "Like seven. Nearly eight." Not since Cory. And they had practiced extra-safe sex, with Tori on birth control, a strict adherence to condoms, and Cory's tendency to pull out.

With Brett, it might not make sense, it might go against everything she had been taught, but if they only had a few times together, she wanted to luxuriate in the erotic friction of skin on skin.

"I haven't done this with anyone but myself in a year," he said, "and I got tested first."

She chuckled. "Sounds like we're covered."

"Or uncovered, as the case might be."

His lips met hers again. A sweet spiraling tugged low in her belly as he uncurled her hand from his erection and lifted her wrist above her head. Her body arched. He raised her other arm and clasped both wrists. She moaned. His mouth lowered to her breasts, and the wetness between her legs budded into a sensitive knot of wanting. Her hips thrust upward.

He inched his fingers southward and rubbed. Flares burst behind Tori's eyelids. She gasped.

"Hurry, Brett. Please." Before she crested and soared.

A sensual haze engulfed her mind and body as he plunged deep inside with a throaty growl. The fastest, most intense rush of pleasure she had ever experienced rolled through her in tumultuous waves. Brett joined her on the wild ride, head lowering after several heartbeats to rest on her shoulder.

"That was amazing," Tori whispered.

"*You're* amazing." He scattered light kisses across her mouth.

Her eyes stung. *Oh, Brett. My Brett.*

But not *her* Brett. Never again her Brett. Not in the way she had once craved.

She would break down his walls and help him become whole in the short time remaining in his stay before they embarked on rich, but necessarily separate lives. Because she couldn't allow herself to fall for him again. That way lay madness. She was boycotting madness.

"We can be amazing together whenever you want, Evans," she whispered, voice shaky. "For two weeks. Until you go."

***

"Mmph," Brett mumbled around a mouthful of warm, freshly baked chocolate chip cookie. The most delicious treat he had ever tasted—aside from Tori. "Daisy's class'll 'uv you. These're great."

"Stop stealing cookies." She swatted his hand. "You're as bad as Rex begging for pizza"—she darted a stern glance down at her dog—"which you're supposed to be putting away, I might add. And remember, *John* baked these cookies. I didn't."

Wiggling his eyebrows, Brett licked chocolate from his fingers. "John and Daisy might fall for your tricks, but you and I and Lorelei all know who 'took whisks' with this batch."

"Oh, for—" Tori transferred the last sheet of fragrant cookies onto a cooling rack on the counter.

Brett washed his hands before placing the leftover pizza slices in a plastic container and sliding the box into the fridge. Snug denim shorts with sexy frayed hems hugged Tori's shapely rear as, brushing past him, she turned off the oven. Back at the counter, she pressed a finger onto a cookie.

He cozied up behind her. Hands on her hips, he peeked over her shoulder. "I see how it is. I can't have another cookie, but you'll pat down every last one, you cute cookie cop."

"I'm testing if the first round is cool enough to pack. Lorelei expects delivery tonight." Stepping away, she adjusted the straps of the pale yellow *Dogs Before Dudes* tank top hanging over her shorts. Tiny paw prints substituted the Os in the phrase.

"Interesting message." Brett gazed at the playful script. "Is it a hint?"

She looked down. "About what?"

"That I should consider Rex *the* man in your life. Until Prince Charming stumbles along."

She smiled. "Rex is ever faithful."

"So am I."

"Brett," Tori responded in a get-serious tone. "You don't do deep relationships. You have friends—"

"With benefits. Agreed." Could that change? With Tori's upbeat influence shaping his perceptions over the next little while, might he learn to expect more from life? "But when I'm dating someone, I'm faithful to her, Tori."

"Of course, you are." Her voice softened. "You're a nice guy, not a jackass cheater."

"I'm the son of a jackass."

Her fingertips grazed his T-shirt. "Your dad doesn't define who you are. Your actions do." She sighed. "I didn't mean to touch on a sore subject. I want to enjoy—whatever this is." She gestured between them. "It's just..." She paused, gaze drifting to the nook table. "...new and unexpected."

"I know." It was downright confusing. He held out his arms. "Come here."

She stepped into a bear hug. Her inquisitive dog lurked at their bare feet as Brett cradled her face and deposited a tender kiss on her mouth.

Earlier, in bed, when she'd mentioned his impending departure, a stab of regret had pierced him. Suddenly, two weeks had seemed too short a duration during which to explore their powerful attraction. Now, as emotions somersaulted and he hugged her close, he couldn't begin to decipher what he was feeling, only that it *was* new and astonishing and perplexing. Tori wanted everything. A husband and kids. A family. Work friends. Community friends. Neighborhood friends. And he wasn't there yet. Someday...maybe?

Wasn't that a sobering conclusion? As a result of his weeks

with Tori, because of the caring, compassionate woman burrowing her nose into his shoulder, he might actually become a better man.

Someday he might be ready for what she needed now.

For the first time in his adult life, the possibility of wanting what she did edged into his consciousness. This feeling couldn't last. It would be cruel to voice his thoughts and potentially hurt her again. He'd come close to revealing too much with his story about the Berlin Wall and that corny statement about her lighting his world. Even if he'd meant every word.

After their incredible lovemaking—he couldn't dismiss the soul-stirring sensations she'd awakened as mere sex—he escorted her into the bathroom for a candlelit dinner in the tub. While they'd enjoyed reheated pizza and zinfandel in acrylic patio wine-glasses, Tori joked that between the unseasonably scorching weather and the hot water, Brett was trying to cook her. Which had led to him teasing her about 'having' her for his next meal. They wound up kissing and caressing, and lathering each other's bodies.

Then he jockeyed for a more comfortable position to accommodate his growing arousal. His elbow bumped the pizza box, knocking slices onto the bathmat and sloshing wine into the water. Citing a need to bake Daisy's cookies, Tori ended their water games. They changed into shorts and cool tops, and she'd let in Rex. The dog had been underfoot since.

"How do you feel now?" Brett asked, smoothing his fingertips over the silky tendrils of hair at her temples.

"Better, except...no offense, I'm getting a headache. It's not you. It's this horrid heat."

"Where are the fans?" Once upon a time, her parents had stashed a collection of standing fans in a corner of the basement workshop for these rare bursts of blazing temperatures.

"In the attic." She smiled. "Let's dig them out."

"Lead the way." He trailed her up the stairs to Ry's old attic bedroom. As Tori opened the door, Rex bolted inside.

Tori's nose wrinkled. "Ugh. It's stuffier in here than the other day with John." Switching on the light, she picked her way between boxes and cloth-draped furniture. "The fans are around somewhere. I spotted them when Dad and I stored my stuff."

Brett wiped his palms on his cargo shorts and glanced around the cluttered attic. Ry's old posters of bikini-clad models and sports cars decorated the slanted ceilings. When they were kids, Marty Jarrett built a new roof and constructed two gables, expanding the original space to create deep pockets on either side of the room. Ry's bed had occupied one pocket while his desk and a small couch inhabited the other. Then, blinds shielded both gable windows and the original pane overlooking the backyard. Tonight, unfiltered early evening sun spilled inside the area, illuminating dancing dust particles.

"I'll open a window," he said.

"Crank all three."

He squeezed between boxes into the right gable and opened the first window. A whoosh of marginally cooler outside air fluttered over his T-shirt. Batting a cobweb, he crossed to the other gable and cranked.

"Find the fans?"

"Over here." Tori tugged open the original window located at the rear of the house. Resting her hands on the sill, she poked out her head and inhaled. "That's better. I love this view."

"What view? The alley?" Brett stepped around a sheet-covered dining set to join her. The fans stood several feet to their left. Rex snuffled along the base of the wall, as happy as if he were tracking rabbits. "I see trees, your mom's gardens, the garage. Backyards across the alley." He counted rooftops leftward. "My old house." Heaviness snaked a fist around his heart and squeezed.

Tori clasped his hand at their hips. Their fingers interlaced. "Does seeing the place make you sad?"

He summoned a smile. "A little." He hadn't searched out his boyhood home during one of his neighborhood dog walks for a reason. His father had acted like a dick in that house. Had irreparably damaged their family in that house. Had betrayed Brett's mother and set up Brett to believe any guy named Hennessy "Hank" Evans or Brett Hennessy Evans wasn't capable of normal, mature, genuine, authentic relationships.

Vanquishing bitter memories, he nudged Tori's shoulder. "Then I remember how great my mom was...your brother the best friend in the world...you...hassling me."

"Yes. Well." Pretty pink washed her face. "I had a bit of a crush."

His smile widened. "Did you now?" *Tori + Brett 4-Ever* flashed into his mind. "Um, I should tell you when I found your notebook I noticed writing inside your desk."

"You looked in my planner?" Her eyebrows arched.

"No, no. I didn't snoop everywhere."

"I hope not." Her fingers wriggled free of his grasp. Her arms folded beneath her breasts, obliterating *Dudes* on her tank top. *Dogs Before* rounded along with her cleavage.

Brett stuffed his hands in his pockets. "The felt marker? The pink heart? Tori and Brett...forever."

"Oh, that. Ha-ha. Scribbled during a weak moment. Teenage angst doesn't count."

It didn't?

"Now I just want you for sex." Tori gazed out the window again. "I love these trees. Don't you? Especially the big maple. It's one of the reasons I bought this place."

Brett followed her gaze. A chestnut tree spread huge, foliage-thickened limbs near the detached garage. The giant maple towered closer to the house while two smaller species he couldn't identify lined the right fence.

"The maple is perfect for a tree fort." A wistful note mellowed her voice. "For my kids."

"Kids?" He swallowed.

She smiled. "I hope my future husband loves old houses as much as I do because my dream is to raise our family here." She stared at Brett.

He slicked his tongue over his teeth. "What are your plans for this room?" How many ankle-biters did she and CHAD intend to produce? One? Two?

Turning around, she leaned her palms against the windowsill. Her gaze cast around the large space. Brett mimicked her stance. Hot evening air flitted over his spine.

"This room would make a perfect combination bedroom/playroom," she murmured after a moment. "Summers are getting hotter. Before I have my babies, I plan to install central air."

"It's a big room for one kid."

"Ry never complained." Her fingers splayed in front of them. "I see...two children sharing this space. My old room is fine for a nursery or third child, but if I had two little boys or girls, I'd want them together up here."

Three kids? Brett's eyes widened. CHAD was a fertile bastard.

"You'll find the right man," he said like a supportive sap.

"Just not now." Her arm bumped his.

"No. Not now." She belonged with him for the next two weeks. After that—

He couldn't bear to think that far.

A sassy smile bowed her lips. "It won't be hard to find the right guy."

"Not at all." What man wouldn't want to settle down with the most remarkable woman in the continental US? And most likely beyond?

Pushing away from the window, she spun to face him. "The hardest part about finding the right guy," she said huskily, lowering her hand to his shorts, "is knowing where to look."

Arousal kicked him in the gut. "I thought you had a headache."

"You're my special medicine. It's gone." Her fingers moved. "*There's* the hardest part."

"Tori." Groaning, Brett angled his head in the direction of the beagle snoring behind a recliner. "The dog is just over there."

"I've heard you get used to having pets around when you… you know." She whispered near his ear, "Suck it up, Evans. I have a hankering. It's here on the dining table or…" Her tongue flicked over his earlobe. "…no more cookies for you." Her hand skittered away from his shorts. She walked backward until the rears of her thighs bumped the sheet-draped table. Planting her hands behind her hips, she hefted herself up. Her legs opened. A spot of faded denim presented itself in all-too-tempting glory.

Good God. He was sunk. "Your mother's dining room table— do you have no shame?"

"Not a speck. It's my table now, and it needs…christening." Rocking back her hips, she unzipped her shorts and shimmied the denim down her toned legs and off her bare feet. Twirled the hem of one leg hole around a finger like a striptease artist and let the shorts fly. Panties tinier than her bikini bottoms barely covered her sweet spot. She curled a finger and beckoned.

Brett grappled to assess the situation. Hours ago, they'd determined they didn't require condoms. No running around scrambling for protection. Just going for it. Being with her. Wonderful her. Amazing, incredible, fascinating her.

Drawing in a deep breath, he stepped between her spread thighs and did what any red-blooded American male would.

He sucked it the hell up.

11

_____

STRETCHING ON THE stepladder, Tori rolled primer onto the wall above the fireplace. The unbearable heat had decreased in the two days since she and Brett had desecrated the heck out of the dining table in the attic. Afterward, their backs and knees sore but their libidos sat-is-*fied*, they'd both grinned like fools carrying the fans downstairs. Brett had set up one in her bedroom and another in the living room, where the blades stirred cool streams of air. The husky timbre of a Marvin Gaye classic glided from the boombox phone dock. The slow, easy beat of the sultry music matched Tori's rhythm as she swept the primer left and right before rolling up and down.

The third fan occupied either Brett's bedroom or the kitchen, depending on his and Tori's…um…needs. As in Brett didn't need to sleep alone any longer, but Rex did.

Luckily, the pooch worshipped Brett and had staked a claim to the shirt-strewn pet cushion in the second bedroom. As long as

Rex's napping spots carried Brett's scent, Brett and Tori were good to go. And go. All night. Every night.

A smile wreathing her face, Tori descended the ladder and ran the roller in the tray. She couldn't seem to stop smiling lately. For once, she and Brett weren't fighting their attraction. They were giving in and getting...it...*on*. Her plan to nooky the man from her system, if initially a trifle harebrained, was taking shape. Brett should have followed her lead from the start.

A door banged. Footsteps echoed in the kitchen. Abandoning the roller, Tori glanced at her dad's chunky handyman watch. Four p.m. Brett Hennessy Evans—Workaholic of the Year—had come home early on a Friday? Who else could it be?

Heart galloping, she tidied her ponytail and adjusted the bill of her baseball cap. *Yes*, every cell in her body chorused as he strolled into the living room, the epitome of hottie-office-casual with his hands stuffed in his trouser pockets and his shirt collar unbuttoned. A grin broader than her own tipped his sexy mouth.

"No fair," he said without a trace of ire, glancing at the primed wall around the picture window. "We agreed to start tomorrow. Saturday. As a team."

"Sorry. Val said my head was in the clouds all afternoon, so I might as well go home. She and Nolan are on shift tonight."

"Daydreaming? You?" Brett teased. "About what, I wonder?"

"About whom is more accurate." About *him*.

Chuckling, he unbuttoned his cuffs and folded back his shirt-sleeves. The soles of his shoes scrunched the clear plastic sheets protecting the hardwood. "You beat me to the punch, starting the undercoating. I wanted to surprise you."

"Ta-da!" Tori bounced on her sneakers. "You're surprised instead."

"I sure am." Reaching her, he curved both hands around her upper arms and pressed a quick kiss to her lips. "Mmm." Palms sliding down and spanning her hips, he pulled her close.

"Brett. There's primer on my top."

"Ask me how many cares I give."

He kissed her thoroughly and deeply while Marvin Gaye crooned about how sweet and wonderful life could be. A longing tugged low in Tori's belly. Life *was* sweet. Tastier than warm apple pie topped with butterscotch-swirl ice cream. An inner voice piped up that if only things were a bit different—like if another man happened along in the not-too-distant future...after Brett returned to Sacramento with a healthier work-lifestyle balance in hand...a man like Brett but *not* Brett, a man who charmed and cherished her and turned her on yet also yearned for a family— could life grow infinitely sweeter?

Then his lips moved on hers again, his hands caressing her waist and hips, and she punted her worries into a murky corner of her mind. Why focus on trivialities while this incredible guy kissed her? Why not live in the moment? Go for the *yi-yi*-triple-*yi*?

Her fingers sifted through the short hair at his nape, and she settled in for an unhurried exploration of his mouth. *Oh, Brett. My Brett.*

Yes, her Brett.

For now.

By the time their mouths drifted apart, their breathing shallow and foreheads touching, Marvin Gaye had given way to a fast-paced Motown girl-group melody. Brett clasped Tori's hands and, threading their fingers, kissed her knuckles. A fluttery sensation swooped in her chest.

"You certainly enjoy a wide range of music," he said with a heart-melting smile as the girl group commanded their listeners to stop in the name of love. "When I walk in the door, I never know what to expect." His index finger rose from their clasped hands. The blunt fingertip stroked her face cheek to chin. Tingles danced on her skin.

"The Retro Vibe might need to focus on music more and more as the years pass." Tori's breathless voice sounded nothing like her usual, take-charge self. "Nolan is curating playlists to catch me up." She attempted a casual shrug. "No one knows what the future holds in the creative industries. Movies, music, and books are rapidly changing."

"Because of tech geeks like me." Brett's blue eyes clouded.

"Hey." She swung their clasped hands back and forth, level with their thighs. "Technology benefits the world. There's room for tech and retro. Hi-fis were cutting edge in the sixties. Now they're vintage. It's not so bad. We all grow and change." Or should. Including her. Not just Brett.

"I know. But don't you ever wish life didn't have to be so—" He glanced around, brows puckering as if he searched for the right word. "Hurry-scurry?"

Tori moistened her lips. "Yes. But the same idea applies. Hurry-scurry isn't inherently wrong." She smiled at his unique turn of phrase. The man had quirks. She loved that about him. "It's part of life. Anyone's life, whether they're techy or not. It's a matter of prioritizing who or what you hurry-scurry for." A man to love. A caring home. Hearts open to exploration and possibilities.

His gaze cut to the fireplace. "I understand. I think I do. I dunno. Maybe I don't. I'm trying to learn." He looked at her again. "Sometimes I feel this itch…"

"Not in your pants, I hope."

He laughed. "No. For something simple. Maybe a little old-fashioned."

"A county fair?" she joked, not wanting the mood to grow overly serious and lead them down a path which might plant them at a crossroads, facing a choice neither needed to make at this early juncture. Not when what they finally shared glittered, sparkly and vibrant, like a jewel beneath bright display-case lights. "Cotton candy? A sack race? Or is a sock hop more your style?"

His mouth slanted. "I sound stupid, don't I?"

"Not at all." She swung their hands again. "I might have something a little old-fashioned up my sleeve. There's a neighborhood block party Sunday afternoon. Want to go?"

"You mean one of those outdoor shindigs your parents hosted every few years?"

"Look at you, hitting the bull's eye in a single guess." Tori squeezed his fingers. "If we finish the undercoating tonight, tomorrow we can paint two coats, leaving Sunday free for the party. You're invited...as my guest."

"I sense a hitch coming on."

She couldn't slip anything past this wily one. "The party is at your old house. A family named Hamilton lives there. Their son Cale is a friend of Mick's, who has Rex right now, if you're wondering where my dog is."

"I thought that T-shirt hog was in my room."

"I needed him away from the paint." Tori chewed her bottom lip. "I realize you have bad memories associated with that house. If you don't want to attend the party, I understand." She would participate regardless. She couldn't miss the annual block party her first year as a neighborhood home owner. The selection of next year's host occurred during the festivities. She wanted in on that community action.

Brett's gaze shuttered. "It's just a house. I won't fall apart if I step in the yard." He sounded unconvinced.

"It *is* just a house. Not a representation of your family. Not anything to do with who you are now."

"Well, Ms. Freud, if you're going, so am I. No one said knocking down emotional walls was easy. If I have to endure memories of Hank at this party to spend all weekend with you, game on."

❧

Three hours later, Brett climbed down the ladder in the hallway and rested his cutting-in brush on an empty yogurt container of primer. "When is Mick bringing back Rex?" he asked Tori as she rolled the undercoat onto the lower half of the opposite wall. Her curvy rear wiggled in her paint-splattered sweatpants.

She glanced over her shoulder. "What're you gawking at, buddy?"

"Uh…"

A grin split her face beneath the bill of her *Keep Portland Weird* cap. "Mick texted when you were in the bathroom earlier. Rex is staying with the Radfords tonight."

"Staying?"

"A beagle sleepover. Mick ran into John and Daisy while he was walking Rex. She begged her dad to keep the dog overnight. I couldn't say no to that sweet little girl."

Lending out a dog? Brett had never heard of such a thing. "That's unusual."

"Not really. Lorelei and I have done this before." Balancing her roller on a tray, Tori sat back on her haunches. The filmy poly sheets crinkled. "Lorelei keeps kibbles and a chew toy in her pantry. Daisy has wanted a puppy for months. John thinks adopting a rescue dog a year or two old instead might help ease Daisy into her role as big sister next winter. They'll babysit Rex a few more times before visiting a shelter."

"Babysit? Big sister?" What other neighborhood news had zoomed over Brett's head this week?

Excitement spilled out of Tori, shining in her eyes and bubbling in her voice. "Lorelei is pregnant! And John got the job! Everything is working out for them, Brett."

"Tori, that's great!" Her enthusiasm washed over him in a joyous wave. "I didn't realize they wanted another kid." He was of the shotgun-wedding variety himself. Hank had made that clear several times during his childhood. If Hank hadn't accidentally 'knocked up' Brett's mom, the man wouldn't have been saddled with raising a 'snotty-nosed brat.' Whenever Hank had wanted to cut Brett's mom to the quick, he would hurl those cruel words. The blistering piece of crap.

Tori nodded. "They've been trying for years. Lorelei has fertility issues. She said I could tell you."

"Fertility?" Brett parroted. A weird sensation slithered up his neck. He might not want kids—at least not until recently, when he'd begun considering the possibility of having a family in a safely nebulous *someday*—but he'd taken it for granted he possessed the proper plumbing and superb swimmers. Olympians. Of Greek god caliber, really. Capable of performing the butterfly while spinning on their...heads?

"You ever worry about infertility?" He couldn't imagine Tori childless or at the mercy of the adoption process, although he knew she would pursue the latter avenue, if necessary. She would do anything to make her dreams come true.

"I *hadn't*. Until now." She retrieved her roller and whacked the end on his forearm. Undercoating sprayed his skin, and the tart scent tickled his nostrils. "Lordy-*Lou*."

"Why, you—" Sexy, kissable spitfire. "You did that on purpose. This isn't cookie dough," he stated in a mock-stern voice. "It's paint."

"Which washes off." Eyes twinkling, she brandished the roller. "Beware."

Lifting his hands and pasting on a terrified expression, he backed away and repositioned the stepladder on the far side of the bathroom door. Climbing up, he resumed cutting in around the door and ceiling. Tori applied primer on the drywall surrounding the front door, where he had previously trimmed and coated the highest areas.

Brett waited until she appeared absorbed in her work. Then, after skimming excess paint off his brush, he crept down the ladder and tiptoed across the protective sheets, barely wrinkling the poly with his off-the-charts stealth. He dabbed the brush to her shoulder blade. She twirled around and squealed.

"I heard you, you know." Her chin pointed. "I didn't realize you were armed."

"I'm sorry," he said and then mouthed, *Not*. "I am sorry I made you worry you're infertile."

She rolled primer up his chest. "That's a bridge I'll cross if I ever encounter it." She deposited the roller on the angled tray. Her gaze flew to his crotch. "There's a lump in your pants." Her lips curled in an impish smile.

"Look at the bright side. It's not an itch. Of the medical variety, at any rate."

She tugged the waistband of the saggy painting pants he'd found in her dad's collection of workshop apparel. "Are you worried?"

His brain fogged. "About your fertility?"

"About yours." She inched a finger into his boxer-briefs, towed open the underwear…and peeked.

"Not at the moment." He tossed his brush onto the roller. "Emergency woody. I can't work in this condition."

"Excuses, excuses. Next thing I know, you'll be starting a union."

"I'm proposing immediate action."

"No voting?"

"You can file a complaint later."

She stuck her nose in the air. "*I'm* the boss."

"Uh-huh." Fitting his palms to her rear, he hoisted her up. Her legs wrapped around his waist.

Minutes later, both of them naked in bed, Tori sexy and beautiful beneath him while a standing fan whirred in a corner, she gazed into his eyes as if he were the only man in the galaxy. And beyond. As if he, Brett Hennessy Road Warrior Evans, was enough.

No woman had ever looked at him with that heady combination of warmth and wonder. Only Tori. Always Tori.

She nourished his soul.

And filled his heart.

۶

"Tori, do you have a free hand for the fruit medley?" Ruby Hamilton asked.

"Hm?" Tori gazed at the Hamilton family bulletin board adorning a kitchen wall of Brett's childhood home, a remodeled four-square with a wide staircase in the middle. Notes, school awards, and printed photos covered the framed cork alongside a chalkboard menu, multiple to-do lists, and schedules personalized to each mini-Hamilton. The paper planner and future mother in Tori swooned. "Sorry, Ruby. I got distracted." She accepted a bowl from the forty-something redhead and balanced the container atop her contribution of chilled pasta salad. "Your children are beautiful. I love the picture of Ellie at her piano recital."

"Thanks. Dan calls the cork my Brag Board. He's always after me to tidy it."

"Why should you?" Marina Traymour's brown eyes sparkled. "Every mom is proud of her babies. Right, Tori?"

"Tori doesn't have kids yet, Rina," Ruby replied, stepping around Lorelei, who was putting the finishing touches on a platter of pickles, onions, shredded lettuce, and tomato slices. Ruby collected the platter and a condiment basket.

Marina poked Ruby's arm. "If she stays in this neighborhood, she'll have babies before she knows it. I swear it's like a disease. I got pregnant with Brandon the week we moved in."

Lorelei washed her hands at the sink. "And look at John and me. Try, try, try for years. Then we move here, and wham. It's magical."

Marina's head swung toward Lorelei. "I heard your news the other day. Congratulations!"

"Thanks. I can't tell you how happy we are."

Tori followed the chattering women to the front entry, passing

Brett's old bedroom—ten-year-old Ellie's room now, complete with a pink-bedazzled tablet and a unicorn stuffie on the bed.

As the group exited the house, Marina's oldest boy raced across the lawn, scowling. "Mom! Brandon's bugging me."

Marina smiled as the dark-skinned boy caught up to his big brother. "It won't kill you to play with him, honey." She knelt on the lawn to speak to both kids.

Tori, Ruby, and Lorelei continued to the serving table in the driveway. Clusters of lawn chairs crowded the front yard, and three barbecues barricaded the walkway from the street. The mouth-watering scent of grilling burgers wafted on the warm air as four men in shorts, tees, and aprons guarded the flames, among them Marina's husband, two fellows Tori had yet to meet, and Brett.

He tipped his beer toward her in a cheer, a ready smile brightening his handsome face. Tori set down the bowls and wiggled her fingers in return. From the instant they'd arrived at the party, it had become painfully apparent they were the only unmarried adults present. The oddballs in a couple-packed world.

But that was okay. She and Brett weren't headed anywhere substantial. They just *were*.

Lorelei placed hamburger and hot dog buns on the table. Ruby, arranging the condiments, gestured toward the barbecue brigade. "Your Brett seems nice."

'Her' Brett was a fantasy. In ten days, he was outta here. Who knew when she might see him again?

"You should keep him around," Ruby added.

Lorelei grinned. "I agree. I mean, look at her face, Ruby. It's obvious."

Tori scoffed. "Obvious?" Jitters pranced in her tummy. Where the heck had they come from?

"How you feel about the guy." Lorelei gave a knowing nod. "When you look at him, your face glows. Frown all you want, my friend. You're still glowing."

Ruby chuckled. "Maybe she's pregnant."

Tori choked. "It's sunstroke." Anything but Brett-stroke. "We're friends." With benefits on the verge of expiring.

Lorelei's eyebrows rose. "You feel a whole lot more for that man than you're willing to let on."

Tori shot her friend a death glare. An instant later, Daisy, playing with Jenny, stumbled on the asphalt, scraping her knee. The little girl plopped onto her rear end and cried.

Lorelei gasped and started toward the pair. Ruby clutched Lorelei's arm.

"Don't, Ruby," Lorelei said. "John is helping the teens out back, and Daisy's hurt."

"Shh. It's a small scrape. Brett is handling it. Look."

Ruby pointed. Brett had plunked down his beer and zipped out from the barbecues, scooping Daisy into his arms and tickling her ribs as she giggled, the minor scuff forgotten.

"Aww," Lorelei and Ruby and Tori cooed.

A flood of love—dazzling and brilliant and intense—crashed into Tori. Brett would make a wonderful dad. Sadly not to her kids, but to some other incredibly lucky woman's. When he was ready. When he accepted what her neighborhood friends realized.

That he was a natural. That he was much, much more than Caring, Hard-working, Attractive Dad-*and*-husband material.

Honest, steadfast, sexy, funny, and a bit offbeat, he was the sort of guy any woman in her right mind would snatch out of the friend zone, given half a chance.

Brett Evans was the real deal. Not an acronym. Or a pale substitute. And she loved him.

The truth rooted in her heart. She loved Brett. Had she ever stopped?

"Daisy's hero," Lorelei murmured.

Ruby rubbed Tori's shoulder. "Miss Don't Know He's Special, meet Mr. Potential Daddy."

Tori sighed, chest aching. How could she have been so blind?

And eager to deceive herself. What could she possibly do about this bone-deep love saturating her body? It was unmanageable. Rioting throughout her cells. Storming in her veins.

Lordy-Lou on a bleeping *yi*, she'd thought she'd had it bad for the man at twenty-two. Four years later, he had spent a mere three weeks in town and love gushed from her pores. It was sheer lunacy.

Brett cradled Daisy against his chest and strode toward Lorelei, who arrowed toward man and child, arms outstretched. Brett transferred Daisy to her mom. His gaze roamed to Tori. Her breath caught as he strolled in her direction.

A gray-haired man intercepted his progress. "Hey, there. Brett, is it? We need trashcans from the side of the house. Can you help?"

"Sure thing." Brett ambled alongside the senior, head ducking toward Tori. "Cute kid," he murmured, and her heart flopped about like a dying fish. She gazed after the men rounding the house, disappearing from view.

Tori + Brett 4-Ever.

In *her* dreams.

Oh, woe.

❧

"Enjoying yourself?" Brett asked Tori over a slice of Marina Traymour's delicious rhubarb pie. They sat in lawn chairs a short distance from a larger group. John, Lorelei, and Daisy had vacated the other seats in their cluster, providing Brett time alone with his beautiful housemate. Something was bugging her, and he aimed to find out what.

She nodded, smoothing a hand along her shorts. "It's been a long day. I'm tired."

His fault. Their plan to paint the living room hadn't proceeded as scheduled. Yesterday morning, they enjoyed leisurely lovemaking before showering together and walking Rex. And then having lunch. And making love again. Around three, muscles sore from the previous day's priming, they finally summoned the will to apply the first coat of a peaceful sage green, which had required drying overnight. They'd painted the second coat this morning. Brett had volunteered to complete the job, but Tori had insisted on doing her part. The poor girl was worn out.

Balancing his paper plate on one knee, he whispered. "Tonight we'll sleep, nothing more." A warm breeze flitted over their shoulders. Leaning close, he swept hair off her face.

She blinked. "In the same bed?"

"Without giving in to temptation. Yes." He skipped a fingertip down her arm. "I want you, sweetheart. I'll always want you. But even sex gods need their rest."

A diminutive smile tipped her lips. Throat tightening, he continued, "I can't think of anything more wonderful than holding you throughout the night, Tori-mine. That is, if you want to share your bed a whole night..."

Her lashes fluttered, the irises glossy.

"Tori?" Were those tears? "Are you okay?"

"Yep. It was an eyelash. Handled." She returned her attention to her dessert, all nonchalant and focused on delivering pie to her mouth—as if he hadn't just risked the most romantic words he'd ever uttered to a woman.

Didn't she realize her profound effect on him? Encouraging him to dig deep and discover the soft insides of a guy who had never challenged himself to reach for more in life?

This morning, in bed, she'd brought up his dad again, suggesting he should contact the man before returning to California. And damn if he wasn't entertaining the notion. Taking his time about it but not dismissing the concept out of hand.

Would she go along if he asked? Make a day out of driving to Salem? But what would taking Tori accomplish? Hank might not act himself with the grown-up version of the cute little Jarrett girl present. For that matter, would Brett? If he connected with his father, he needed to face the man alone, not employ Tori as a buffer.

They finished eating. Brett gathered the plates and dumped them in a trashcan near the barbecues. Clint Traymour glanced up from scraping grates.

"Brett, my man! How's it hanging?"

"Exceptionally well. You?"

Clint laughed. "Same." He pointed his scraper at two burger-laden plates on the side shelf. "Cale and Mick asked for double cheeseburgers for dessert. Teenage appetites, huh? Those were the days. Eat heaps and not gain an ounce."

Brett nodded. "Can I help?" Throughout the party, he'd fended off memories of the bad old days by assisting Tori's community troupe wherever needed.

"The grills are under control. But take the food? The boys are out back. Thanks."

Brett carried the plates around the house, glancing over his shoulder to glimpse Tori pretending not to watch him. A grin tugged his lips. He would miss her. So much. He couldn't say that about any of his former friends with benefits, not even Kendall. Sharing an apartment for months with the driven attorney hadn't dislodged a single brick of his protective facade. A few weeks with Tori had changed him somehow deep inside.

He toed open the unfastened gate and entered the backyard—his post-divorce refuge. Where he and Ry had played Twenty-One at the hoop, camped out in a pup tent in the pouring rain one soggy summer, and gabbed endlessly about girls and life. Those had been the *good* old days.

He surveyed the property. Either the Hamiltons or another previous owner had constructed an expansive deck and replaced the tall privacy fence, but the colorful flowerbeds hearkened back to Brett's mom. Blossoms spilled over the five-inch-high rock wall he'd helped build. Terraced levels rose behind the main beds, and a basketball hoop jutted from the detached garage. New hoop and siding but same spot, Brett noted as he headed for two college-aged teens throwing bean bags at cornhole boards. Hip-hop music drifted from a window. The other kids must have retreated indoors.

"You gotta make your move, Mick," a strapping redhead who could only be Cale Hamilton said, chucking a bag at a football-themed board. It missed the hole by an inch.

"I wanna, dude." Mick, a lanky type with one arm in a sling, jumped off a sneakered foot. His sack sailed neatly into its target.

"Maniac Mick!" Cale high-fived Mick's good hand. "Ten bucks says you won't. She's too old for you, bro."

Mick ran a finger along the bristles dotting his upper lip. "What's seven years when she's hot and she wants it? That's how I busted my collarbone, yo."

Cale slapped his thigh, chortling. "You fell off a stepladder!"

"I was staring at her ass. She's babysitter-*fine*." Mick flicked a tank top strap, and sub-zero ice crackled on Brett's face.

The arrogant twerp means Tori.

The burger plates fell to the lawn. Brett's fingers hardened to stone. *"Excuse me?"*

The teens turned, leaping back.

Cale's face went white. "Brett—Mr. Evans—I didn't mean—"

"I don't have a problem with you, Cale. It's this guy." He stared down Mick. "That's how you talk about a woman whose worst crime is being nice to you, *yo*? What girl wants to be with a guy who treats women like chunks of meat? You think your mom deserves respect from your stepdad, don't you? Or is she a joke to him?"

Mick's tough-guy bravado disappeared. "Don't talk like that about my mom!"

"Then don't speak that way about Tori. Or any other woman. Show a girl you like—someone your own age, not an adult running a business—what you have in here." He patted his chest. "That's who she wants to see, Mick. Not a strutting rooster."

Mick held up his good hand. "Awright. I get you. Don't tell Tori I said anything, 'kay? She's cool. And I really like walking her goofy dog."

"I won't if you treat her and every other woman in your life with respect from now on. I'll be watching you, Mick. Don't forget it." Brett piled the slipshod burgers back onto the plates. He shoved a burger toward Mick. "Here's your dessert. I suggest you eat."

12

BRETT'S ENCOUNTER WITH Mick bothered him throughout the workweek. By Thursday he'd developed the irksome habit of staring at computer screens and seeing nothing. Mick was young and stupid. His offensive remarks about Tori were only to impress Cale. He would mature and learn. The kid wasn't destined to become a carbon copy of Hank Evans. Brett hoped. But the similarities ate at him.

Was that why he bristled whenever Tori mentioned Mick? Seifert reminded him of his dad. And maybe even of himself.

He grunted, gaze boring into the Sugartree monitor. Who was he to lay into a nineteen-year-old college dude about treating women with respect? Had he respected Tori by vanishing from her life four years ago? They had discussed that night multiple times. It was dealt with. But it didn't feel behind him. It was like a scab itching on his skin. Primordial ooze festering in his brain. He couldn't slap on a bandage or kick dirt over scabby ooze forever. Could he?

Because that sounded a helluva lot easier than examining his personal failings over and over.

"Earth to Brett." Fingers snapped above his ears. "You in there?"

Brett swiveled in his chair. "Greg." The Sugartree Information Services manager. "What can I do for you?" He picked up his mug and sipped his mid-morning coffee.

"It's what I can do for you." Greg smiled. "Colleen and I are having a friend for dinner tonight. She thinks you two might hit it off. Want to come? Coll's lasagna is fantastic."

"A woman?" Brett affected a neutral expression. "I'm leaving next week. Kind of late in the game for a blind date." Plus, what about Tori?

"Just offering you the chance for some R and R. She's a lawyer. Great girl. Kendall Brandt."

Brett spewed coffee onto the desk. Dark spots pelted papers.

Greg clapped his shoulder. "Be careful how you swallow that crud."

Coughing into a fist, Brett parked the mug ten inches from his keyboard.

"She's not against a long-distance thing," Greg added.

No, Brett imagined she wasn't. "I don't do long distance." Until Tori. He couldn't just say so long and expect her to serve as his port in the storm the next time he flew to Portland to check in with Sugartree. They needed to develop parameters for some sort of ongoing romantic relationship. If she wanted one.

Therein lay the billion-dollar question. How many weeks or months was she willing to devote to knocking down his walls before she got fed up and resumed her search for Mr. Right? Was it fair to ask her to devote any time?

"The invite is good for another hour," Greg said, sinking onto a chair and flipping through a sheaf of hard copy. "Coll needs to hit the grocery store."

Brett cleared his throat. "To tell you the truth, I'm dating someone. So tonight won't work."

"Yeah? Good for you. Didn't mean to put you a tight spot, buddy."

"You didn't." Brett tapped a mechanical pencil upside-down on the desk. "Listen, I'm heading out. I'll come in this weekend to make up for it."

Greg sniffed an armpit. "It's not me, is it?"

Brett laughed, pushing back his chair. "No. My dad lives in Salem, and we've had trouble coordinating our schedules," he fibbed. "If I don't visit today, it could be months." Or never. Tori's observations about Hank had rubbed off, it seemed. She had given Brett a second chance. He would learn from her stellar example and do the same for his father.

"Go." Greg's hand scooped the air. "Family is everything."

Maybe for an upstanding man like Greg Lawson. Definitely for people like Tori, Ryan, and their parents. Brett's mom and her husband Keith. The Radfords and other neighborhood families.

Brett, on the other hand, needed to work on the concept.

Tori's head pounded as if a Transformers movie thundered inside it. "Will that be everything?" she asked Mrs. Kirk, who had temporarily set aside Chris Hemsworth to binge Mark Wahlberg.

"Yes, my club members will be overjoyed. Next week it's back to Chris, if I have my way." The woman slid large sunglasses onto her nose. "They can have their Marky-Mark. I need my Aussie fix."

Tori forced a smile. Mrs. Kirk left, and Meridy stepped close.

"Hey," she said in a quiet voice. "You're not your usual chatty self. Is something wrong?"

Aside from this bear of a headache? "That depends on how you look at it."

Meridy's gaze widened. "Oh, my God," she whispered, brows

shooting up. She checked the vicinity of the cash desk for customers, but most appeared engrossed in browsing selections for the flash record sale announced in the store's newsletter. "You did it," she whispered again. "Slept with Brett for closure. Did it work?"

Tori leveled her friend a sardonic look. "Closure is for fools, Mer. I belly flopped into the deep end of the pool. Now I'm drowning."

Meridy's fingertips flew to her mouth. "Oh, no."

"I love him," Tori whispered. "He's leaving in six days, and I'm nowhere near over the guy. I don't know if it's possible. I just keep sinking." The metaphorical water rippled above her head, and the stench of too much chlorine stung her nose. The lifeguard perched on a tower, gaze tracking little kids and old folks, completely missing Tori going under.

Meridy clutched Tori's hands and squeezed. "Tell him."

Tori snorted. "I love him," she repeated beneath the din of a movie playing on an overhead monitor. "This isn't 'like,' Mer. Or infatuation. I'm in love with the man. I am doomed."

"You are not." Meridy smacked the counter. "You are Tori Jarrett. You are never doomed." She poked Tori's chest. "You pick yourself up like no one else I know. You're my best friend. I've got your back, and so does Val. We will not let you crumple into a ball over Brett Evans ever again. Tell him how you feel. What do you have to lose?"

That he would break her heart again. It would split in two this time, with jagged edges like in a country music song, and she would never recover. She would crawl into a corner, bury herself in dogs and cats, become the neighborhood crazy lady, scare the kids at Halloween, and take up knitting.

That was her future.

❦

The answer to the question of how Brett had grown into a

dunderhead about women when a devoted mother had raised him sat across the table in a seedy strip club buried in the bowels of beautiful Salem. A silicon-enhanced dancer gyrated on stage as Hank studied the lunch menu. His bald scalp gleamed. Did the man buff his pate to a shine after shaving off every stray hair?

Sounded like Hank. With a broad chest and solid biceps, Brett's father, at fifty-five, remained in excellent physical shape. An Evans Concrete logo stretched across Hank's red T-shirt. The same design emblazoned an extended-cab four-by-four parked outside the club. Hank had said his years in Alaska had served his company well.

"Find anything you like?" Brett asked, pressing a thumb onto the laminated paper. The odor of stout and stale pretzels permeated the air.

His father's eyebrows bobbled. "Plenty." Leering, he angled his chin toward the stage.

Brett resisted the urge to groan. "I meant from the menu, Dad."

"Still uptight as your mother, I see."

Still rude and self-centered, I see.

Fingers twitching, Brett refused to rise to his father's bait. Hank had sounded taken aback when they'd connected via cell during the hour's drive to Salem. An Internet search in the Sugartree parking lot had produced the Evans Concrete website, a photo of Hank's smug smile and faded blue eyes, a business address, and mobile number.

Before Brett could change his mind, he'd directed his rental car toward the I-5, and Hank, supervising an active work crew, picked up the call en route. Hank hadn't been obligated to drop everything on short notice in the middle of a busy Thursday to see Brett. Were the man's vulgar comments for show?

A bored-looking server sidled up to the booth. Brett ordered nachos.

"Hot wings." Hank rolled his shoulders. "Or is breast on the menu?"

Brett cringed. Hank was certainly predictable.

"Hot wings, it is." The server yawned. "Want another beer?"

"Make it two." Hank veed his fingers. "We're celebrating. My son decided his old man was worthy of a visit. Coulda' shown his face a little sooner, but I'll take what I can get. Am I right?"

The server arched her eyebrows, stretched her jaw, and slinked off.

"So," Hank said, swigging his beer before glancing at Brett, "how's the consulting biz? Jetting around the country fixing everyone's code. What? Don't look surprised. Your mother told me. Still based in California?"

Nodding, Brett tapped his fingers against his frosty glass. "Work is good." Although this latest assignment—or, rather, the bevy of surprises that had occurred during it—had him reevaluating everything. He dug DataPrimer, but, in the end, it was just a job. Something to fill his days and nights and the empty pieces of his soul. Returning to Portland had opened his eyes. Next week, while he laid low in his apartment for a few days like some software efficiency superhero awaiting a bat signal, it was Tori he'd miss. Tori he wanted. Tori he loved.

Heart pounding, he shifted on the hard wooden chair. He loved Tori. Not as a pal or childhood friend or someone to broaden his emotional horizons, preparing him for a possible someday with someone else, but as a sexy, sassy, lippy, cheeky, know-it-all, give-it-her-all, beautiful woman.

Other men might realize they'd fallen in love during a romantic stroll on a sandy beach or as heated bodies joined in ecstasy, but he experienced the epiphany in a peeler bar while the dancer curled around the pole like a snake sliding along a jungle vine and his old man insulted the server.

"You're in contact with Mom?" he asked, chest and mind

burning with the realization of his feelings. He pictured Tori, hands on hips. *"Took you long enough,"* she'd mutter.

Hank shrugged. "Now and then, your mother and I talk. How else am I to keep tabs on my boy?" He reached across and thumped Brett's forearm. "Your Ma..." Hank hemmed and hawed. "Nice gal, but not really my type. Now, Leanne, my last lady—what a handful. Know what I mean?" He cupped his fingers on his chest and simulated squeezing a woman's breasts. "If you want my advice—"

Brett didn't.

"—spread your seed with a matronly sort but then set your sites on a quality Leanne," Hank finished in a jovial, let's-be-macho manner.

Brett's stomach roiled. "Are you and Leanne still together?"

"Nah. But that's okay. One set of hooters is as good as the next."

Brett's jaw firmed. "I'd rather not talk about hooters," he stated in a tight voice. "And I don't want to hear any more belittling remarks about Mom."

"Who has the big vocabulary? Take it easy, son. Just having fun. When's the last time we lazed around and chugged a few?"

"Never."

"Then let's start. Not another word about hooters. Or seeds. I promise." Hank lifted his palms in mock surrender.

The server arrived with the nachos and wings. "Beers a-coming," she drawled, setting down the plates.

Brett stood and plucked several bills from his wallet. "I have to go. I'll catch you on the flip side, Hank." He dropped the cash onto the table.

"That's it?" The man's eyes creased. "I thought we'd spend the afternoon together."

"Something's come up." If Brett lived nearby, perhaps with time and a truckload of therapy, he might break through his sperm donor's Cro-Magnon posturing and discover a variation of a father figure beneath.

But not today.

❧

Meridy peeked into Tori's office. "Feeling better?" her BFF asked.

Tapping keys, Tori closed the bookkeeping program on her desktop. New entries chugged from the printer. "A little."

After Nolan came on shift, she'd walked to the nearest drugstore to buy pain reliever. The thumping in her temples had diminished, but now a raw knot twisted her stomach. She didn't have the slightest idea what to do about Brett.

Meridy closed the door to a crack. "I have to tell you, Tori, you don't look great."

"Heartache does that to a person."

"I know." Sympathy brimmed in her friend's gaze. "Brett called the store while you were gone. Nolan answered. It's been so busy, he just told me. He said Brett rang your cell, but you didn't answer."

"It ran out of juice, and I got bogged down here." It was a brain-burp kind of day. "Any message?" She accessed her phone charging on the far side of the computer tower. A missed call from hours earlier displayed.

Meridy nodded. "Brett drove to Salem to visit his dad."

"He did?" Tori itched to dash off a text and ask how it was going. But she'd only disrupt the men. She put down her phone. "That's wonderful." The Hank Evans she remembered didn't deserve a remarkable guy like Brett for a son, but for Brett's sake, the relationship needed to heal or, at least, achieve some form of closure so he could move on.

Where had she heard that before?

She chewed the inside of her cheek, running a finger over her phone screen.

"He'll be home late," Meridy said. "Why not take advantage of this time? Leave Brett to work things out with his dad. Or not. What happens in Salem is up to them. Go home, cuddle Rex, and journal your feelings. You might gain a fresh perspective."

"I can't." Fear tickled the back of Tori's throat. Her choices seemed clear. Tell Brett she loved him and face potential heartbreak, or ride out their arrangement and embrace the next chapter of her life solo. "The sale is motoring. You and Nolan will need me."

Meridy tipped her head. "I thought you'd say that."

The office door opened, and Val strode in, wearing a Retro Vibe top. "Ditto."

"Hey." Tori got up. "We changed the schedule. It's your day off."

"Not anymore. Meridy called. Tori, I know you're scared but jump in and see what happens. Don't stress over how Brett might react to the wonderfulness of your love. Wade can be a real ass at times—in fact, he's in fine form today, so coming in is a break for me—but I love him anyway."

Meridy's gaze grew misty. "We can't help who we love."

"But we *can* help what we do about it," Val contributed.

Tori shook her head. "You two are ganging up on me? Forcing me to face my feelings?"

Val's lips pursed. "Aren't you clever?"

Tori smiled. She had the *best* friends.

Brett tugged the leash. "Rex, come on. It's a walk. By definition, you need to keep putting one paw in front of the others."

Snout buried in a flowery bush, the beagle practiced selective deafness and sniffed the greenery. Checking his pee-mail, as Tori would say.

"Rex." Brett pulled again. The hound lifted a leg and sprinkled his mark before dashing ahead of Brett on the sidewalk, the retractable cord spinning out like a fishing line. Brett provided the dog six feet of slack. Rex trotted to the next yard and parked his nose in a shrub. Brett groaned. He knew when he was beat.

"Okay, buddy. You win." It was a beautiful afternoon. Why hurry? He had cut short the Salem trip to allow himself the luxury of processing the reality of falling in love while the object of his affections remained occupied with the LP sale. Brett had suggested the discount as a way to reward Tori's email customers as well as attract walk-ins, and she'd run with the concept. He admired her willingness to take risks, her resourceful business sense and creative imagination. He adored her sassy mouth, the sparkle in her thickly-lashed eyes, and, *oh, mama*, he worshipped every inch of her curves. The heady sensation of her beneath him, above him, around him. Her heated touch and sexy glances.

But, most of all, he felt safe with her. He no longer felt alone.

He yearned to share these incredible feelings. Now that he'd wised up and realized what was happening, romantic protocol dictated he should tell her how he felt. But he couldn't blurt out a declaration. He needed to prepare. Now he had time. Glorious hours stretched ahead.

The dog's ears perked. Rex glanced up, brown gaze curious.

"Go ahead, boy," Brett said magnanimously. "Have at her."

The beagle inspected individual leaves as Brett rocked on his wingtips, drinking in the blue sky, the far rolling hills, and the puffy clouds framing snow-capped Mount Hood. He stood almost mesmerized, absorbing the quirky vibe of Tori's city and neighborhood. His hometown and the stomping grounds of his youth. The temperature hovered around a balmy seventy-two, an improvement over last week's heat. His inner Oregonian approved.

Rex padded to the next yard, and Brett ambled along, inhaling invigorating breaths. This could be his life. Walking the dog with

Tori. Working on her house. Maybe *their* house one day, if he was lucky.

Stroking his chin, he nodded. He'd banked a lot of cash over the years. Enough to contribute to the renovations and the office space above the store, helping Tori achieve her goals much earlier than anticipated. They would marry—

He swallowed. Yes, he was going there. His mind was really going there. They would marry...in about a year. Before she turned thirty, they'd try for a baby. Say in three years, perhaps two, to lessen stress about infertility. They'd have an adorable little boy or girl, not a screaming infant. Although, he supposed all newborns hollered on occasion. No problem. He would deal with it.

The idea of having children terrified him even as excitement rippled beneath his skin. He had never honestly considered becoming a father. He had never truly dreamed.

This could be his life.

A butterfly with yellow and black markings frolicked above Rex's head. The merry dog leapt and snapped his jaws, narrowly missing a wing.

"Rex!" Brett yanked the leash, and the swallowtail fluttered away unscathed. That was close. "No treat for you," he scolded, directing the dog to the lane behind Tori's house.

A vibration in his pocket indicated an incoming text.

Bzzz. A second text.

Bzzz. A third.

He pulled out his cell.

Tori: *I can't find Rex!*

Tori: *Have yo see Rex?*

Tori: *Did yu tk rex to salem???*

Damn it. Brett texted, *Have dog. Near house. On walk.*

He tapped a second message: *Sorry. Didn't think.*

Tori: *Thank God!*

Tori: *Where r u?*

Brett dialed her cell.

"You have him?" she answered, tone agonized.

"Yes. I thought you were at the store." He quickened his pace. Rex strained toward a fence. Brett glanced down and whispered, "Help me out, boy. Tori is worried. You want a lap? Your lap is at home." A nap on Tori's lap—Rex's recreational drug.

Rex scampered down the lane, matching Brett's brisk strides.

Tori sobbed. "Brett, you never take a beagle out of his yard without leaving a note! Once a hound catches a scent, he could be lost for hours. Overnight!"

"I understand. But that didn't happen." He had checked every fence board ages ago, confirming the safety of the dog's spacious corral. "Rex is with me. He's fine."

"But your car—" She inhaled on a tattered gasp. "It isn't here. How was I to know?"

Good question. "We're in the lane. We're nearly home. I parked in the garage."

"You parked in the garage?"

He never parked in the garage. "I wanted to see what it felt like."

"To park in the garage?"

"Yeah." When he'd returned from Salem, he'd lifted the ancient metal garage door, climbed back into his rental car, and concealed the vehicle within the structure, pretending he performed the routine daily. He had collected Rex and set off on their walk, imagining himself and Tori strolling the lane arm in arm for decades to come. No longer kids or awkward teenagers but as adults in a mature, loving, committed relationship.

It had felt fantastic until her frenzied texts rolled in.

"Brett, he's my dog. I think of Rex like my baby."

"I know." Now more than ever. "I screwed up. I'm sorry. We're seconds away." Staying on the line, he stepped toward the open gate. Tori stood near the unkempt carrot patch, eyes wide and hair disheveled. A young mom carrying a toddler flanked her left, and the senior Brett met at the block party cupped her opposite elbow. The three adults stared expectantly. The child drooled.

Brett's heart sank like an anvil propelled off a cliff. Tori had organized a search party for her dog. Because of his ineptitude.

Crrapp.

🙚

Lordy-Lou-Lou-Lou!

"Oh, my God. Thank God." Kneeling on the grass, Tori unleashed Rex. The cord whizzed into the handle Brett held. Rex jumped against her jeans, licking her face. "Next time, please call or text," she said in a hushed voice.

"Or leave a note. Got it." Slipping his phone into his pants pocket, Brett glanced from neighbor to neighbor. "Thank you for your concern. You can go home."

"Brett," Tori whispered, standing and digging an elbow into his ribs. Honestly, he sounded abrupt. She painted on a polite smile. "Jodie and Logan"—she flourished her fingers toward the mom and two-year-old—"were headed to the playground. Howell"—she motioned at the senior—"was enjoying iced tea on his patio. They heard me calling Rex"—actually shouting and bellowing the dog's name—"and popped by."

How had Brett not caught the racket of her panicked voice jetting at eardrum-splitting decibels throughout the neighborhood? Howell lived five houses away, and he'd heard. Like a whistle on the wind, the older man had noted.

She shook Howell's hand. "Thank you for your concern." Chucking Logan under the chin, she said to Jodie, "You can go home."

The neighbors departed. Tori turned with Brett toward the porch. Rex followed.

"I freaked out when I couldn't find him." Similar to the afternoon she'd discovered Brett handymanning her house. Except worse. "Sorry if I sounded snippy."

"You had every right. He's your dog."

Tori winced. She loved this man. How was she to tell him now? *Dude, I just ripped you a new one but not to worry, I'll probably do it again. You know, if you want to stay in touch after this. So you might as well get used to a little impromptu freakage. Or you can run for the hills and never return. Oh, and by the way, I love you to bits.*

She required a smoother transition. Maybe another day to ponder her next move.

"How did things go with your dad?" she asked as they entered the kitchen. Rex romped to his eating area and stared into the empty food bowl, brown ears drooping.

"Not awful. Not fantastic. Not somewhere in-between. I'm not saying there isn't hope. You have taught me there is always hope. But I can't salvage the relationship on my own."

Tori's insides warmed. She had taught him something? *Aw.*

"At this point, I'm not sure I want anything to do with the guy." Brett's mouth curved downward. "He's the same old shallow Hank, and he hurt my mom a lot."

"He hurt you plenty. Take a few days. See how you feel then."

Brett sliced a hand lengthwise through the air. "I don't want to talk about Hank." A dramatic flair deepened his voice.

"Okay." Drawing out the word, Tori curled her hair behind an ear. "What do you want to talk about?" Her heart beat a rapid cadence. A curious tension bubbled between them. Her fingers shook. "Wait a minute. I need to feed Rex." She portioned kibbles into the bowl, and the dog danced at the dish. Facing Brett, she adjusted her shirt. Skimmed her hands over her bare forearms. Swallowed. "Ready."

His blue gaze rested on her face, his lips tilting upward.

Get the lead out, darn bovine, she instructed telepathically.

"I'm moving to Portland!" He swept out his arms.

"What?" Her eyes bugged.

"Back to Portland, I should say. I'm moving back. I love you, Tori. I want to be with you."

"W-wow!" Her legs wobbled, and prickly patches itched on her skin. For years, she'd imagined Brett Hennessy Evans proclaiming his undying love. She had fooled herself these last few months spinning fantasies about CHAD. She had almost settled for Close Enough with Cory. But Brett Evans, the man standing in front of her at this very moment, speaking words her younger self would have given anything to hear, was the guy she had always wanted.

As a teenager dreaming about her older brother's best friend.

As a twenty-two-year-old eager to divest herself of her virginity.

And now, four long years later, he had finally spoken the words. So why wasn't she throwing herself into his arms?

"I had an epiphany in Salem." Brett clasped her hands. The pads of his fingers glided over her unpolished nails. "I love you, Tori. I want you. I want Rex. I want this house. This neighborhood. A life with the best person I know. I want it all."

Her heart badda-bumped. "How can you want all of that all of a sudden?" *How can you want everything I do?*

Joy shone in his clear blue eyes. "It's been happening this whole time. Since I walked into your living room as clueless as you said. And I'll gladly own that. I was clueless." He caressed her fingers. "I realized my feelings today, but they've been poking me for weeks. You're my sexy little cattle prod."

Tori blinked. Love had poked him? Like a cattle prod?

"You're beautiful and amazing and wonderful." He brushed a kiss across her lips. "This is where you say you love me too."

"I love you, Brett. I have for years. It's a lifelong condition. But I'm scared." Her throat squeezed, and tears burned the backs of her eyes. How could she express her darkest fears and risk ruining this precious moment? Brett gazed at her as if he floated on a love high. She recognized the expression from every time she'd glanced in a mirror after running into him years ago. But she needed to put her insecurities out there. If they were going to give love a go, she couldn't hold back. "Love means always being there for someone. And I don't know if you can just climb the highest tree around and swan-dive off."

"But I have." His lips stroked her mouth. "You achieved the impossible. My walls are down."

It would be so easy to fall into him. To bask in today and not worry about tomorrow. "Your life is in California."

"A speed bump we'll smooth over."

"I want to believe that. So much." Placing her palms on his chest, she forced herself to say, "What if you wake up tomorrow, or the next day, or next week, or next month, and realize…" She inhaled. "…you've made a mistake? I can't ask you to give up everything you've built in Sacramento and then walk on eggshells, wondering if you might leave again."

His forehead crinkled. "You don't believe I'm in love with you?"

"I do." She wanted to. "But your feelings are very new." He'd only added two plus two today.

"You don't trust what I'm feeling. You don't trust me." He stepped back.

"It's not a matter of trust." Her pulse blipped in the hollow of her collarbone. "Neither of us is perfect."

"I'll say." He shook his head curtly. Rex sank onto the floor and whined. "I understand we'll fight, Tori. That doesn't mean I'll walk. Walking away from you four years ago was the stupidest thing I have done in my life, bar none. But I had my reasons."

"I know you did. We both showed bad judgment. That night is behind us."

"If that's true, then let's be happy we've found a way back to each other. Be happy with me, Tori."

She clapped her chest. "I want to."

"But you doubt me. My walls are down, and yours are going up. I'm laid bare. I'm exposed, and you're stacking bricks to the sky." Pain contorted his face. "Isn't this the height of irony?"

"Brett." She reached for his hand. He jerked away. "I love that you love me." Hot tears seeped from her eyes. "But we aren't playing house. I come with future baggage."

"You mean having kids? Gee, I hadn't thought of that. Guess I lack the capacity."

"You must admit, it's a turnaround. And it's not an area where I can compromise."

His brows lifted. "Apparently, I hadn't considered that either."

He had considered raising a family? Deep in his heart, not while soaring on a love high?

He was giving her everything. What was she giving him?

"But do you really want this?" She gestured wildly around her work-in-progress home, where she had plotted to sleep with him, never dreaming that getting over this man was impossible. He had become part of her, imprinted on the essence of who she was. "Living in the neighborhood where your dad cheated on your mom and hurt you in a thousand ways? I'm sorry if that sounds harsh, and I'm not an immovable block of stone. I can't budge on having kids, but I can adjust in other ways. As long as I know what I'm getting into."

"Tori, I swear, you make me lose my mind. Life isn't a neat-and-tidy to-do list I can write out in precise order. I've peeled away every painful layer of skin to show my heart to the woman I love, and it's not enough. You still believe I'll hurt you."

She flinched. He was right. She was a coward.

"I think it's best you go." She hugged her ribs. "At least, for a little while." She needed a clear head. Whether he realized it or not, so did he. "I want to be alone."

He snorted. "You got it." He grabbed his laptop case from the counter. "I should have stuck with the hotel arrangements. Instead of trying to fix us, I should have listened to you and stayed far away."

"I'm glad you didn't," she whispered.

"Well, glory be." His eyes iced over. "Take note, I'm not running from anything." He flung open the porch door, gesturing at Rex to stay. He looked at Tori. "This time, love of my damn life, you chased me away."

*rett's Cell Phone ~ Notes App*

- *Wrap up Sugartree*
- *Return rental car*
- *When life throws you a curveball, hit it out of the damn park*

BRETT HUNCHED ON the edge of the hotel bed, fingers laced on his thighs and thumbs circling. His room service meal sat untouched on the table, his open laptop beside the plate. In a matter of hours, his life had changed—and not for the better. How had he allowed this afternoon with Tori to spiral out of control?

He loved her with his whole heart. He yearned for the life he had envisioned sharing with her today. Now that the switch had flipped in his brain, there was no turning back. He needed family. A dog, a cat, a couple of gerbils. Two or three kids with their mom's warm hazel eyes and glossy brown-sugar hair. Friends and a community. A different career. He itched to build and create. To no longer scrutinize code.

Assisting with Tori's renovations had reawakened his enjoyment of physical labor and jumpstarted memories about the construction squad he and Ry had gabbed about developing as kids. If Hank hadn't worked in an offshoot of the housing industry, Brett and Ry's vision might have grown to fruition. As a young teen, Brett hadn't wished to emulate his father in any manner. Without consciously realizing it, had he focused on advancing his computer skills as another way to separate himself from Hank?

Deciphering code had enthused him since childhood, and for years, he'd loved his job. Unfortunately, the intricacies of his career had driven him to achieve and achieve and achieve. To the point where he had become an achieving machine and, before these weeks in Portland, not much of a human being.

Tori lay at the heart of his clarity of purpose. He needed to convince her he was here for good.

He stood and strode to the hotel window. Hands on hips, he stared at the parks and green space adorning the cityscape. His cell phone vibrated on the table. Forehead puckering, he answered.

"Mom. Is everything okay?" They seldom spoke after ten p.m. Florida time.

"Just jim-dandy here, honey. How are you?"

"Great." That was a colossal stretch. Brett narrowed his gaze. Why was she asking?

"Now, Brett," his mom intoned. "I spoke to your father. I understand you saw him today."

"I left early. Did he complain?" Brett had yet to process Hank keeping tabs on him 'now and then' through his mom. It felt odd.

"I wouldn't put it that way," his mother replied. "He's worried he put you off."

"Well, you know him." Brett wouldn't repeat the

conversation.

"I do. Hank is a tough nut to crack, hiding behind that macho wall. He wants a relationship with you, but—"

"Same ol' Hank," Brett filled in. "Mom, can I ask you something?"

"Of course."

"What did you ever see in the guy?"

Brett's mom's musical laughter chimed in his ear. "Hank was quite a charmer in his day. Handsome, enough muscles to turn a girl's head, quick with a joke. When you came along, he wanted to try—I'll give him that. We both did. We weren't the best match. Deep down, I think I realized it wouldn't work out." She paused. "I don't regret building our family, honey. That's how I got you."

"I suppose that's something." Brett shrugged.

"You bet it is. I wouldn't trade you for anything. I had this fantasy about Hank that plays out on greeting cards every Father's Day. It was foolish of me, really. But, you know, in the end, my time with your father led me to Keith, and he's a gem." She paused again. "Here's some motherly wisdom. Some leopards can't change their spots, and I suppose Hank is one of them. Brett, be a leopard who can."

"I would love the opportunity." Dragging his fingers through his hair, he described the confusion over his rooming arrangements, Tori's renovations, and a splash of their romantic complications.

Pleasure brimmed in his mom's voice. "That's wonderful you and Tori have hit it off. She had a thing for you as a teenager." His mom chuckled. "Smart girl. Persistent. And patient, it seems. Wonderful traits. Will you continue seeing her after you return to Sacramento?"

"Mom, you don't understand. I want to share my life with her, but I blew it."

His mother pshawed. "Then unblow it. What other choice do

you have? Go get her!"

Mothers. She made chipping away at Tori's wall sound simple.

"She's stubborn," he mumbled.

"And you're a catch. Show her how much of one you are. Leave her no room for indecision."

Rubbing the back of his neck, Brett looked around the hotel room. Maybe his mom was onto something. Without a doubt, he didn't want this life anymore. He refused to isolate himself, and he couldn't let Tori close a literal or metaphorical door in his face ever again. He would do whatever it took to prove himself. If she didn't want him, tough. He was here to stay.

"Thanks, Mom." He smiled. "Unblow it. Someone should inscribe that on a Father's Day card."

"Yes! I'm in your corner. Let me know how it goes."

They ended the call. Brett breathed in and out, heart thundering against his ribs, excitement racing in his veins. He wanted to change his life. Not only for Tori but for himself and their future family.

He sat at the hotel table. Rolled up his shirtsleeves. Pushing aside the room service plate, he opened his email program and clicked his best friend's address.

❧

Tori stood in the hallway door to her childhood room, gaze moving from Brett's things on the dresser, to a sock hanging out of the partially full hamper, to the handball on the bed. Rex snoozed beside the toy, nose tucked into his tail, as if patiently sleeping away the time until his favorite human returned.

Except it looked like Brett wasn't coming back. Not to say goodbye to the forlorn beagle and not for his stuff. A heavy weight crushed Tori's breastbone. She had torpedoed the best scenario of her life—Brett saying he loved her. Two days ago, he'd stormed out of her house with only his computer case in a tight grip and the office clothes on his ultra-fine frame. He hadn't sent a single text, and neither had she. What did you message a man you'd asked to leave moments after he'd peeled open his heart? Did you say, "Hey, dude, I miss you like crazy." Or, "Sorry, sweetie. I was a twit." Maybe, "You shocked the hell out of me." Or, "Sorry. So, so sorry." Or, "Come get your stuff, and let's talk." Or, what she really wanted to say, "Come. Just come. Please come back to me."

Eight times yesterday and at least fifteen this morning, she'd typed and deleted a variation on the same theme into her phone. Several times, she'd dialed Brett's cell and promptly hung up, reasoning that if he needed to torture her with the frostiest shoulder on the continent to recover from the pain she'd inflicted, shouldn't she respect that decision?

But then, minutes ago, she called the front desk of his hotel near Sugartree to discover he had checked out. Today. Had he finished his contract early? Was he skipping town—again— because they'd hit a bump?

Her *life* was bumpy. If Brett wanted to climb onto this partic- ular roller coaster, he needed to accept the lows as well as the highs. She needed to invite him to join her on a crazy ride. They would plunge but they would also soar. Together.

Plucking her phone out of her shorts pocket, she spun into the hall and paced to the front door, the hardwood cool on her bare feet. She had made a stupid choice on Thursday. Brett was the love of her damn life, and they deserved a chance at happiness.

She tapped his name. The call went to voicemail. The digital recording played. "Evans. Brett Evans. I used to like it shaken, but now I like it stirred. This message will never self-destruct. All is well in Whoville. We'll always have West Berlin."

Tori gawked at the phone. References to James Bond, *Mission Impossible,* Dr. Seuss, and *Casablanca*? Hardly a professional greet- ing. What was he thinking?

The beep sounded. She placed the phone to her ear. "Brett, it's me," she said in a tiny voice. "I wouldn't blame you if you never wanted to see me again. But I love you. I do. I love you." Tears spilled down her cheeks. "I need to tell you in person. You can laugh in my face, throw your martini at me, storm my walls, whatever you need. I have to see you. Please call me back."

Shoulders hunching, she thumbed the red icon.

Whack! Whack-whack-whack!

The familiar sound of hammering jolted up her spine. Hand to her throat, she cocked an ear.

Whack-whack!

She ran into her old room, accidentally bumping the bed and jostling Rex. She peeked out the window. *Brett!* Wearing jeans and a pale blue T-shirt, he hunkered beneath the large maple tree, nailing two-by-fours together. Lumber and a sheet of plywood rested on the grass.

"Rex!" She thumped the bed. "He's here!"

The dog launched off the mattress and tore ahead of her into the kitchen. Rex body-slammed the doggy hatch. His legs and tail disappeared through it in a blur. Clutching her phone, Tori opened the door.

Brett welcomed the dog beneath the majestic maple tree. "Hi, boy." He laughed and dodged a sloppy tongue. "I missed you too."

Howling his approval, Rex vaulted over the lumber and sprinted massive circles around the yard.

Tori stepped onto the cool grass. "I—I left you a message." Plush blades sifted between her toes.

"I hope it was good." Brett patted a pocket. "Felt the vibration, but I was busy." He inclined his head toward her phone. "Heard from your brother yet?"

"Ryan? He's—"

"Been checking email these last few days. A lucky break for me."

"What do you mean?" Tori's phone rang, and she glanced

down. "This isn't his number."

"It's temporary." Brett's chin lifted. "Go ahead. Answer the damn phone. I'll wait."

He wanted her to speak to Ryan rather than discuss their issues? Lips wobbly, she placed her faith in the man and answered the damn phone. "H-hello?"

"Tori?" Her brother's voice crackled over the poor connection.

"Ryan!" It felt so good to hear from him. She darted a questioning glance at Brett. He shrugged and crossed his arms, a determined man of mystery. Tori asked Ryan, "Where are you?"

"Guam now. Seventeen hours ahead of you. It's early Sunday here. Listen, Shrimp, I'm touching ground stateside in three days. Tell Mom and Dad when you talk to them tomorrow, all right?"

"Oh, my God! You're coming home early?" Happy tears dampened her lashes.

"Because of Brett. I should beat him to a pulp for falling for my little sister, but I love the guy like a brother." He laughed. "Guess that sounds incestuous."

Tori dashed quick fingertips beneath her eyes, wiping away the moisture. "Um…"

Ryan said, "I know him better than anyone else does, except for maybe you now. Hear him out. He won't do you wrong."

She didn't require Ryan's relationship advice. "I was planning to hear him out. I was planning to talk to him."

"Give him first go then, okay?"

Maybe she could accept Ry's advice this one time. Emotion clogging her throat, she nodded.

Brett's head angled. Stepping close, he peeled her fingers off the phone. "Let me borrow this for a second." He pressed a quick kiss onto her lips. Confusion, love, and heat flooded her veins.

"Hi, Ry," he said into her cell. "I've got it from here…Yep. Thanks, buddy, I agree. It's gonna be awesome." He chuckled. "Yeah, yeah. The left pinky finger first, if that's all right…It won't come to that. Put my dismemberment out of your mind."

Ending the call, he tucked the phone into Tori's hip pocket. His breath tickled her neck as his hand lingered on the curve of her waist. Tingles whispered along her skin.

"What's going on?" Her voice emerged as a raw whisper. A silver-gray pickup sat in the alley, the tailgate down. A large box depicting a cast iron table saw rested in the truck bed along with more plywood and assorted supplies. Rex stopped running circles and sniffed the ground by the maple tree.

Brett clasped her hands. "I know I wasn't supposed to contact Ryan while he was away, but I needed to talk to my best friend. I spoke to your mom and dad this morning too. Every Jarrett in the Pacific Northwest—at least the ones I've met—knows what I'm up to. If today goes south, so be it." Gaze tender, he murmured, "I understand we're not playing house, Tori. Sweetheart, I'm here for life. Want to hear more?"

Unable to speak, she nodded.

"I meant it when I said I'm quitting DataPrimer. The Sugartree staff doesn't need me anymore. I'm so efficient, I optimized myself out of a contract." A smile tipped the outer corners of his mouth. "I spoke to my supervisor. I had time off coming anyway. We extended it to forever. I need to make a quick trip to Sacramento to pack some stuff, and then I'm home for good. You can come along, if you'd like. Ry will dog-sit."

Tori's eardrums pounded. "Brett?" *Don't leave me hanging now!*

"Your brother and I are opening a remodeling business. Instead of going out on his own in the construction industry, Ry is partnering with his best bud. That's me." He grinned. "Our first job is those offices above the Retro Vibe. If all four building owners agree, we'll reserve two for our new company." He caressed her fingers. "I need a place to stay until you let me back inside your house, and…I hope…into your heart." He swept a hand toward the maple. "I could live in this tree fort I'm building."

Tori swallowed. "Tree fort?"

"For our kids. I love you, Tori-mine. I'll keep telling and showing you until you believe me."

Another rush of happy tears sprang to her eyes. "Brett, I love you more now than I ever dreamed possible. I adore the tree fort, and I want you to build it, but you can move into the master bedroom any time. I'm lonely there without you. And it's not my house anymore. I want it to be ours."

"Ah, Tori. My love." He enfolded her in an embrace, and they kissed. Lovingly. Tenderly. With mounting passion. When they parted, he cleaned the dampness from her cheeks with gentle swipes of his fingertips and lowered to one knee on the grass. He tugged a sparkling diamond ring out of a jeans pocket. "This is one of the reasons I spoke to your parents. I wanted their blessing before I asked—" He clasped her hand and held up the beautiful ring. "Will you marry me, Tori? Have babies with me? Be my dearest friend and darling wife?"

"Oh, my gosh! A thousand times, yes!"

He slipped the ring onto her trembling finger. Standing, he kissed her again. Rex glanced over as the love of Tori's totally-worth-waiting-for-it life curled an arm around her shoulders and walked her to the maple tree.

He pointed to a lopsided heart in the bark. "I carved this before unloading the two-by-fours. That's how sure of us I was. And am. And will remain until my dying day."

Gaze misting, she read the inscription. "Tori + Brett 4-Ever," she whispered. Gliding a hand up the back of Brett's neck, she kissed her fiancé, her lover, her dearest friend. His benefits would never expire.

"I love it. And I love you. Forever."

"Forever," Brett whispered.

Join Cindy's Email List for notification of new releases
www.cindyprocter-king.com

ACKNOWLEDGMENTS

Thank you, first and foremost, to my husband, Steve, for helping me realize my dreams.

To my editor, Karen Block, for helping polish this manuscript to a shine—and for getting my sense of humor.

Mary J. Forbes, Laura Langston, Jamie Kain, and Brenda Jernigan, thank you all for reading and brainstorming earlier drafts of this manuscript.

Finally, a nod to my dog, yep, my dog, Allie McBeagle, who left us at 16 shortly after I finished the editing stages of *Getting Over Brett*. Allie was the inspiration for Rex, the two-year-old beagle in this story. I'm not sure I could have managed digging back into the book if Allie had passed before I wrote *The End*. So, thank you, girl, for hanging on. Beaglahs forever!

ABOUT THE AUTHOR

Romance Writers of America® Golden Heart finalist Cindy Procter-King writes flirty romcoms, sassy suspense, and heart-warming hometowns. To sum it up, feel-good fiction. Cindy's novels and short fiction are available from eBook retailers all over the world, as well as in trade paperback, library hardcover and large print, some foreign editions, and audiobooks.

Cindy lives in Canada with her family, a cat obsessed with dripping tap water, and the ghost of Allie McBeagle.

Visit Cindy on the Web
www.cindyprocter-king.com
www.cindypk.com

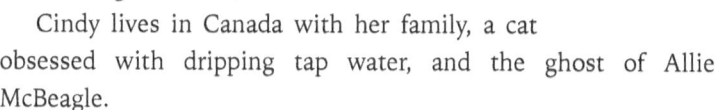 facebook.com/cindyprocterkingauthor

twitter.com/cindypk

instagram.com/cindyprocterking

bookbub.com/authors/cindy-procter-king